DRAGON GUARD CRUSADER

Dragon Guard of the Northern Isles Book 6

ALICIA MONTGOMERY

www.aliciamontgomeryauthor.com
first electronic publication July 2022

Edited by LaVerne Clark
Cover by Jacqueline Sweet
12192022

ALSO BY ALICIA MONTGOMERY

The True Mates Series

Fated Mates

Blood Moon

Romancing the Alpha

Witch's Mate

Taming the Beast

Tempted by the Wolf

The Lone Wolf Defenders Series

Killian's Secret

Loving Quinn

All for Connor

The True Mates Standalone Novels

Holly Jolly Lycan Christmas

A Mate for Jackson: Bad Alpha Dads

True Mates Generations

A Twist of Fate

Claiming the Alpha

Alpha Ascending

A Witch in Time

Highland Wolf

Daughter of the Dragon

Shadow Wolf

A Touch of Magic

Heart of the Wolf

The Blackstone Mountain Series

The Blackstone Dragon Heir

The Blackstone Bad Dragon

The Blackstone Bear

The Blackstone Wolf

The Blackstone Lion

The Blackstone She-Wolf

The Blackstone She-Bear

The Blackstone She-Dragon

Blackstone Rangers Series

Blackstone Ranger Chief

Blackstone Ranger Charmer

Blackstone Ranger Hero

Blackstone Ranger Rogue

Blackstone Ranger Guardian

Blackstone Ranger Scrooge

Dragon guard of the Northern Isles

Dragon Guard Warrior

Dragon Guard Scholar

Dragon Guard Knight

Dragon Guard Fighter

Dragon Guard Protector

Dragon Guard Crusader

PROLOGUE

ABOUT THREE YEARS AGO...

For Lady Willa of the Ice Dragons, there was nothing better than looking outside her window every night before bed. There was something so soothing about staring outside her bedroom window, watching the stars twinkling in front of the vast curtain of the evening sky. And some months, she would be blessed with an even more glorious sight—the northern lights, swaying and waving high above, like a blessing down upon earth. Her people believed, after all, that the Goddess Herself lived up in the sky, watching over them from behind the clouds and the lights.

Once, when she was a child, she had tried to fly up there in her dragon form. But as the air grew thinner and much too cold—even for her ice dragon— she returned to earth. It was much too high for her to reach, or perhaps the Goddess didn't want to be disturbed by silly little dragons like her. After all, She was busy running the world.

So, Willa continued to watch the northern lights from below. It was one of the few things that she was thankful for, living out in the vast bleakness of their homeland, located at the edge of the world.

Though she loved her clan and being an Ice Dragon, part of her wanted to escape Fiorska. The weather was always freezing, being located high above the arctic circle. It made an ideal home for the Ice Dragons, but except for the northern lights, the seasons never changed.

Snow. Cold. Ice. Year round.

She longed to be somewhere she could experience the freshness of the spring air rolling into the heat of summer before cooling into the glorious shades of the fall.

But perhaps she should have heeded that sage old advice.

Be careful what you wish for.

Willa had been looking out of her window when she heard the loud crash and shouts from the lower floors of the Ice Dragons' main compound. *What in the world is going on?*

A blood-curdling scream made every hair on the back of her neck stand on end. Instinct and her dragon told her something was amiss.

Father? she called out through the mind link that connected all dragons of the same kind. *What's going on?*

Stay in your room, he replied, his voice strained. *And hide.*

Hide?

Willa, my treasure, he pleaded. *Do this for—*

The abrupt breaking of the mental link sent Willa reeling back, as if an invisible force pushed at her entire body.

Something was very wrong.

Gilla? Benjamini? Timoteus? If her father was in the compound, usually, at least one of his lieutenants was around. But her calls were met with silence.

Wrapping her robe tight around herself, she didn't even bother with her slippers as she dashed out of her bedroom and made her way to the lower levels. The sight that greeted her as she took the last flight of steps made her heart slam against her rib cage, freezing her to the spot.

Several figures—humans who worked in the compound, lay prone on the ground, as if they were dolls strewn about by a wayward child. Shock washed over her, as well as fear. They couldn't all be ...

"No," she denied, but her enhanced hearing couldn't pick up any heartbeats or breaths. Not a single one. Except—

Father!

At first, she couldn't believe it. Lord Lanz, Alpha of the Ice Dragons, lay crumpled on the ground in the middle of the room, a pool of blood around his body, the red liquid seeping from a wound on his side.

"Father!" She rushed to him, dropping to her knees. "Oh, Goddess, no ..."

The faint rising of his chest gave her hope. "Father ..." She shook him gently. "Please ... Why are you bleeding still?" His shifter healing should have sealed up such an injury. But no, the warm sticky blood continued to flow out.

His eyelids fluttered open. "M-my trea ... sure ..." He gasped. "Run. Run before they find you."

"Run? From who?" she cried. "Father, tell me."

"No time!" He gripped her arm, the burst of energy catching her by surprise. "Run, now! Or they will find you too!"

Willa saw the desperation in his eyes, but there was something else that was not quite right. Like there was something missing.

But what?

"Who—" A sharp pain shot up her spine, growing and spreading across her body like she was being ripped apart. She screamed.

"Vile, shifter scum!" a voice cackled. "You deserve this and more."

Willa felt like she was being emptied, as if her very soul was being torn from her body. Then, a loud crack startled her.

Where did that come from? It was so close her ears began to ring.

When she glanced down at her chest and saw the redness spreading across her white robe, she gasped. Then, her body fell forward, landing on her father's body before the world went black.

The voices woke her up.

"How can we tell her...."

"... gone ... all of them...."

"Monsters!"

It took all of Willa's efforts to even blink. *Weak ... why am I so weak?* At the same time, she felt like she was floating. It didn't feel good, exactly. But it didn't feel bad either. Like she was wrapped up in clouds. However, her brain, too, was foggy, as if it was filled with cotton.

Where am I?

"She's awake."

"What?"

Three figures slowly came into focus as she blinked

several times in an attempt to bring her vision back to normal. On her left was an older man with white hair, and beside him was a younger man. When she turned to the figure on her right, she found herself staring up into blue eyes. They were dark at the edges but grew lighter around the irises. They reminded her of the night sky lit up with stars.

"Lady Willa," the younger man began. "I am Prince Aleksei of the Northern Isles. We met last year at the Dragon Council meeting in Corum."

Prince Aleksei?

Ah yes. Her first trip abroad last year. Quite a trip for someone who'd spent her entire life living in the most isolated place on earth. What an amazing experience it had been, being in the desert headquarters of the Sand Dragons. She'd accompanied her father—

Father ...

The memories flooded back into her mind.

Her father, on the floor. The pain ...

"No!" she shrieked, then shot up like a rocket. "No ..." *Merciful Goddess, please, no. Let it have been a nightmare.* But as she surveyed her unfamiliar surroundings and the expressions of the three men around her, she knew it had all been real.

"I'm sorry, my lady," Prince Aleksei began. "We received the distress call, but as you know, the Northern Isles is a few hours away, and by the time we arrived ... I'm so sorry."

Her father ... all those people ... gone ...

"We brought you back here to recover," the old man interjected. "The bullet missed your vital organs, thankfully."

A sob escaped her throat. "Who else did you bring back?"

The prince's lips pulled back. "Again, I am so, so sorry. There was no one else."

"N-no one?" The numbness started in her limbs, then spread through her whole body. "Th-that cannot be. We have a hundred people living in Fiorska with us. And twenty-six Ice Dragons." Being shifters, they could heal fast and survive even the most life-threatening injuries to humans.

"They were already gone by the time we arrived." It was the third man who spoke, the one with the midnight blue eyes. "I found you, underneath the others. They must not have realized that you were still breathing and had piled them over—"

"No!" Rage replaced the numbness in her, coursing through her veins like wildfire. She leapt out of the bed, managing to take two steps, but the two younger men restrained her. *Why did the Goddess let this happen to me?*

"Please, Lady Willa," Prince Aleksei's grip tightened. "Your wounds—"

"Take your hands off me!" She struggled with all her strength and called on her dragon. "I will take my revenge and—" She gasped as she felt ...

Nothing.

Only a vast, emptiness inside of her. Like a giant crater.

Her dragon. Just ... gone.

"W-what's happening to me?" Her gaze shifted between the three men, searching for answers. "I can't ... why can't I feel my dragon?"

"My lady." The older man guided her back to the bed. "The people who attacked you, they managed to take The Wand."

She felt the blood drain from her face. "No ..."

The Wand of Aristaeum, that foul weapon of their greatest enemy, had been entrusted to the Ice Dragons for safekeeping for the last hundred years. Fiorska was one of the most remote places on earth, after all, and the Dragon Council deemed it safe enough there. If those men had been able to steal it and use it, that means ...

A deep wail rang in her ears, and it took a few seconds before it registered that it was coming from her own mouth.

Her dragon was gone.

She called to it, cried, screamed. Ordered it to appear. But only silence replied to her.

"I'm sorry, Lady Willa," the old man covered her hand with his. Her first instinct was to yank her arm back, but her limbs were locked in place from the shock and grief. "I—" He stopped, the lines on his brows deepening. "The council is here."

"The Dragon Council." As the Alpha's only daughter, she knew of the council that ruled over collective dragon affairs. One day, she would join them, after all. Or at least, that was before ... "I don't want to see anyone else," she whispered. "Don't make me."

"We won't." It was midnight blue eyes who spoke. "You do not have to do anything you don't want to."

Prince Aleksei raised an eyebrow at him, but said nothing. Not out loud, anyway, as they were likely communicating through their mind link.

Another thing she would never get to do again.

The old man cleared his throat. "Aleksei and I will meet with them. Come, my son."

My son?

So, that was King Harald, ruler of the Water Dragons and

the Northern Isles. She should have guessed from the similarities in their appearance.

"We will be back as soon as we can," Prince Aleksei said. "I promise you, we will do everything in our power to make things right."

"Unless you can bring my father *and* my dragon back, nothing can make this right!" she spat bitterly. How dare he make such promises? She was no child. She was Lady Willa of the Ice Dragons. Future Alpha—

She slumped back and closed her eyes. She was lady of nothing, Alpha of no one. *Not anymore.*

When she heard the door slam shut, she opened her eyes again. To her surprise, she was not alone.

Midnight blue eyes peered at her. She expected to see pity in them like she'd seen in the prince and the king's eyes, but to her surprise, there was none. Only curiosity.

"Why are you still here?" she snapped at him.

"I am not needed elsewhere."

She crossed her arms over her chest. "And how long do you plan to stay here?"

"As long as it takes."

Her mouth opened to ask what he meant by that, but she thought better of it and stopped herself.

Of course, she did want to know what he meant, but what did it matter? She had nothing now. She *was* nothing.

And no amount of time would ever change that.

CHAPTER 1

As soon as he spied land from afar, Thoralf knew he was almost home.

Home.

Such a strange thought, this idea of home, especially after two years of traveling the globe. In his time in the outside world, he'd stayed in many kinds of dwellings—from grand mansions to the humblest of huts. But not all of them had been *homes.* No, there was more to the idea of a home than just walls and a roof.

It was fortuitous that today would be the day he came back—Rorik's wedding day. He didn't plan it, but perhaps it was a sign from the gods. His friend didn't know Thoralf was arriving, of course; he did not want the captain of the Dragon Guard to worry, especially today. So, Thoralf decided he would remain Cloaked and watch the ceremony. Only Aleksei knew that he was coming. The news he brought was urgent, but they had already waited for two years, so what was another few hours, especially since it was a special day for Rorik?

Thoralf landed just outside Helgeskar Palace, seat of the king of the Northern Isles. Even after all this time, it was strange to think of Aleksei as king. After all, he was practically a brother to him, having grown up with him when Thoralf became a ward of then-King Harald.

Guilt gripped him, freezing him in his steps as he approached the palace. It was his fault that King Harald had to step down. Thoralf should have protected him that day, when The Knights attacked with The Wand.

It should have been me.

He gripped the satchel in his right hand tightly. Soon, he would make up for his failure. He would restore his king's dragon. At least, now, he had the solution.

Sort of.

There was still one more piece to the puzzle. And there was only one person who could help.

After all this time, her beautiful face remained clear in his memory, despite the fact he'd last seen her as she lay in the hospital bed, recovering from her injuries. His blood chilled each time he recalled finding her, hidden under the pile of bodies. Those were memories he did not dwell on. Rather, he focused on her.

He remembered staying with her as she lay there, staring into the distance. Even when her eyes grew heavy with sleep, he stayed with her, unable to leave.

As long as it takes.

Thoralf didn't know the meaning of his own words. They just ... came out. But he recalled staying in that room until King Harald called for him a few hours later. He could not deny his king after all, but he remembered feeling conflicted. His desire to ensure she would not wake up alone clashed with his duty as captain of the Dragon Guard.

Little did he know he would never see her again after that.

The sounds of a string orchestra playing the wedding march jolted him back to the present. He followed the melody, all the way to the back of the palace to the great lawn that had been decorated for the occasion.

Aleksei, he called. *I am here.*

Just in time, Aleksei replied. *Are you sure you want to wait to announce yourself?*

I am. Let Rorik and his mate have their day of happiness.

All right. When you're ready, just call.

I will, my friend.

Thoralf settled himself in the back, far away enough so as not to alert anyone else with enhanced senses, but close enough so he could observe his friends.

From his viewpoint, he could see Aleksei as he stood on the dais where he would perform the ceremony. Beside him was Rorik waiting for his bride. Thoralf smiled to himself as he saw the Dragon Guard looking around nervously. When Thoralf had handed the duties of captain over to him, Rorik had been confident that he would be up to the task, though Thoralf had to remind him that there was more to it than just leading the rest of the guard. But Thoralf knew he made the right choice choosing Rorik as his replacement, and from what he'd heard, he'd met and exceeded everyone's expectations.

Sitting right up front were the twins. Though they looked exactly alike, they were as different as night and day. The cold, intellectual Gideon never let anyone past the high walls he had around himself, while frivolous Niklas wore his heart on his sleeve. But even though he'd only spoken with them through video chat the last two years, he could tell the two of them had found the middle ground between their extreme personalities. Gideon seemed more loose and carefree these days, while Niklas was more focused.

And finally, towering over all of the guests even as he was seated, was Stein. Thoralf had never known a more serious person, but also fiercely loyal. He was a terror on the battlefield, and just one stone-faced look from him could send anyone fleeing. That's why it seemed strange to see the tenderness on his face as he looked down at the pretty, petite woman next him.

Thoralf suppressed the laugh building inside him and shook his head. Lady Vera Solveigson and Stein? There was no odder couple in existence, yet, watching them gaze lovingly at each other, they seemed like two pieces of a puzzle that fit together. He was truly happy for Stein for having claimed his mate, but even he did not anticipate such an event happening; after all, Stein had even less interactions with women than Thoralf did.

The music began, and the crowd went silent. Thoralf relaxed and watched the ceremony unfold.

Despite not participating in the merriment, Thoralf enjoyed himself as he watched the reception from the sidelines. He laughed at his friends' antics, and for a little while, he forgot his troubles. It was obvious everyone there too—especially his friends—needed the distraction of such a joyous occasion.

Rorik, especially, looked nothing short of radiant as he danced with his bride and laughed with his new stepson. Even from afar he could see the difference in his friend; in fact, he saw it in all of them, and he could guess that had something to do with finding their fated mates.

A deep longing sigh came from within him as his dragon watched its compatriots with envy.

Envy?

Thoralf had never been one to want what others had. He was contented with his life as ward of the king and then later, a Dragon Guard. Did he wish he grew up with his parents? Of course, any child did. But King Harald and Aleksei never made him feel unwanted, which was why it was an honor to protect them. Still, he often wondered what would have happened if his mother and father had lived and he grew up like any normal Water Dragon.

Thoralf? Aleksei's voice interrupted his thoughts. *Are you still here?*

Yes, I am.

The party's mostly winding down, and Rorik said Poppy's ready to head back home soon. I think it's time to let everyone know you're here.

Thoralf slapped his forehead. *I did not realize that, of course ... after the wedding, the bride and groom would want some time alone. Let's wait until morning.*

Aleksei chuckled. *Do not worry about it. Poppy looks ready to collapse after the stress of the wedding week. I'm sure they have nothing planned for tonight except sleep.*

Are you quite sure? Perhaps you should ask Rorik first.

Of course. But we should meet, regardless. Why don't you head inside and wait for me to call you?

I will.

A wave of nostalgia hit Thoralf as he entered the palace, and distant memories echoed in his thoughts. Running down the halls with Aleksei, hiding from the nanny, playing swords and accidentally knocking down that very old vase that used to stand by the staircase—and both of them getting punished for it because Aleksei refused to name him as the culprit. He continued wandering the quiet hallways until he heard Aleksei's voice once again.

I've called everyone to the library. I'll see you there, my friend.

Thoralf made his way to the opposite wing of the palace, taking his time as more memories continued to flood his brain. He wanted to make sure everyone got there before him. They would surely have the same questions, so it would be best to answer them all once they were together.

Thoralf? came Rorik's voice in his head. *You are here?*

The familiar sound of his friend's voice comforted Thoralf. *Yes, I am here. Forgive me for concealing my presence these last few hours.*

There is nothing to forgive, came the booming reply. *But why did you not announce yourself, my friend? You could have joined us for the wedding and the reception, and met my bride and my new son.*

I did not want to disrupt this day—yours and your bride's day, he replied. *Besides, I watched the ceremony from afar, and to me, that is the most important part.*

Rorik did not reply right away, but he guessed it had something to do with the voices he heard as he drew nearer to the library. He paused, waiting for their conversation to play out.

"... I'm not an invalid," Queen Sybil said, her tone obviously annoyed. "And by the way—you weren't going to call me to this 'urgent meeting,' were you? I had to hear it from Annika."

Rorik cleared his throat. "Your Majesties, please. Everyone else has been waiting for this news."

King Aleksei's scowl didn't dissipate, but he nodded anyway. "Call him in."

You heard His Majesty ...

Thoralf took a deep breath.

"Your Majesties," he greeted as he entered and placed his right hand over his heart and bowed. *And my friends,* he added to the others in the room. Aside from Stein, Gideon, and Niklas, the newest members of the Dragon Guard, Ranulf and Magnus were beside them, both of whom acknowledged him with a respectful nod.

"Thoralf!" Gideon exclaimed. "What are you doing here? I thought you were in Antigua?"

"I was," he explained. "But I discovered something over there. Something that may finally bring us the cure to The Wand and defeat the Knights."

"What is it?" King Aleksei demanded. "Tell us."

"I promise, I will." And now was the part he was most reluctant to reveal. But he had no choice. "But first, we must speak to Lady Willa." *Does she still stay at the cottage?* he asked Aleksei.

Of course, the king answered.

Good. Thoralf didn't know why, but he was comforted that she had made her new home in *that* particular place. Something about it seemed so ... right.

"Who?" It was the female dragon who spoke. *Annika Stormbreaker*. Mate to Niklas.

Thoralf met the gazes of the king, queen, and his fellow Dragon Guards. They didn't even need to use their mind link to know what each was thinking—that such a short question required a long and complicated answer.

"We have much to explain," the king finally said. "And I apologize, Lady Vera. You shouldn't have to bear this burden along with us."

Thoralf didn't even realize that Stein's mate was in the room. From what he'd heard from Gideon, Lady Vera had changed a lot in the years he'd been gone.

"I am your loyal subject, Your Majesties," the lady declared. "And your enemies are mine. My duty as a citizen of the Northern Isles is no burden."

Her words surprised Thoralf, as the highborn lady had always been somewhat of a snob who never thought of anyone but herself. But from the way Stein beamed at her, it was obvious that Lady Vera had indeed grown up and changed for the better.

"You should come with us then," the queen said. "Lady Willa will need all the support we can give her."

Thoralf's chest tightened at the words. Finally, after years of roaming the earth, he would finally get to see her.

He only hoped the news he brought would be welcomed.

CHAPTER 2

Willa placed the leather-bound book on her lap and closed her eyes, sinking back into the comfortable chair with a soft sigh.

Nothing like finishing a good book on a cozy day.

She stretched out like a cat and looked outside. *Or should I say, evening?*

Chuckling softly, she got up and placed the book on the table beside her. It was so nice to lose herself in another world. Growing up, she hadn't been a reader. In fact, this was a habit she'd only picked up when—

Her mind went blank, and she went still for a moment. Putting those thoughts out of her head, she strode over to the small kitchen of her cottage and grabbed the kettle, then refilled it from the sink before setting it on the stove to boil.

It's all right, she told herself. Sometimes, she allowed herself to think about the past. Just little glimpses of those days long gone.

Willa closed her eyes. Yes, they were long gone. This was the present. Her life now.

For the most part, she was content. How she loved her little cottage on the edge of the cliff. It was quiet and peaceful out here, and something about this house made her feel comforted. It was a thousand times better than her previous living space.

Soon after she came to the Northern Isles, King Harald had placed her in a special room underneath the palace where she was under watch twenty-four hours a day. *For your protection*, the king had said. She couldn't blame them. When she found out what happened to her father and the rest of her clan, Willa had longed to join them and even attempted to take her own life.

It wasn't until she met Queen Sybil—then Sybil Lennox —when her mate trapped her in the same room to "protect" her from the attackers that Willa had a chance to escape the room. Sybil had used her dragon fire to burn the place down. And while Willa could have used that chance to run away or even achieve her goal of ending her suffering, she found that she just ... couldn't. And so, she stayed behind, waiting in the palace until the fight was over.

And after that and the attackers had been fought off, Willa had been transferred to a remote cottage at the edge of the main island. Prince Aleksei had told her that it was Sybil's wishes that she not be treated like a prisoner under guard and that she could be trusted.

"My mate has faith in you," the then-prince had told her before he left her alone. "I hope you do not prove her wrong."

Despite her hatred for Sybil—because the other she-dragon was still whole while she was not—Willa could not bring herself to disappoint the future queen.

Still, it was too painful for her to see Sybil. She was a

reminder of what Willa had been, and what she had now lost. Months went by, invitations to come to visit, but Willa left them unanswered.

But somehow, Sybil's patience—or perhaps stubbornness—won Willa over. One day, a few weeks after the royal wedding, Willa heard a knock on the door.

"Hello, Willa." Queen Sybil herself stood outside her door like she belonged there.

Shock had Willa staring at her, jaw dropped. "What are you doing here?" She slipped on a chilly mask. "I told you, I didn't want visitors."

"It's been months, Willa." The queen had placed her hands on her hips. "I've been patient with you, but even I have my limits. Will you invite me in?"

"You are queen now," Willa had replied snidely. "And you own everything here, I suppose, even this cottage. I couldn't stop you if you wanted to barge in here."

The queen's expression didn't falter. In fact, she simply smiled. "But I'd rather be invited. Maybe for a cup of coffee?"

Willa had stepped aside. "I'd rather have tea."

Queen Sybil's smile brightened. "Then tea it is."

Willa couldn't remember much of that first day. Perhaps they simply sat in silence while they drank tea. But from then on, the queen would come by every few days, bringing cakes from the kitchen or books from the library. At some point, Willa started looking forward to Queen Sybil's visits. She found the young woman's presence soothing and refreshing and loved hearing her stories about growing up in Blackstone. It all sounded so strange and wonderful at the same time. Also, Sybil never asked her about her own childhood, for which Willa was grateful for.

And so, for the last year or so, they had become friends somewhat, with Sybil coming to visit her at least once every two weeks. Sometimes she would bring Prince Alric as well. Willa enjoyed spending time with the toddler. Perhaps because, like his mother, Prince Alric didn't ask questions about her past nor were they to blame for her present. He was pure and untainted. Carefree and so innocent.

A loud whistle jolted Willa back to the present. Turning off the stove, she took the kettle off the burner.

Tea and a quiet evening alone.

This was her life now, and she was content to spend the rest of her days this way. Ignoring the hollow pit slowly forming in her stomach, she retrieved the tea tin from the shelf, slamming the cupboard door shut. She was reaching for the teapot when a knock on the door made her entire body freeze.

No, it was just my imagination.

The follow-up knock told her that it was, indeed, real.

But why would Queen Sybil visit so late?

Besides, there was some event going on tonight, if she recalled her last conversation with the queen correctly. Why was she here now?

Well, there was only one way to find out. Abandoning her tea, she headed to the front door. Her voice shook as she called, "Your Majesty?"

"Willa? I'm sorry to bother you," came Queen Sybil's muffled voice. "But I need to speak with you. It's important."

"Of course." The urgency in the queen's voice was evident, so Willa grabbed the doorknob.

"Willa, wait, I'm not—"

She yanked the door open. "Your Maj—" Air squeezed

out of her lungs. The queen was not alone. No, several people joined her, including the king and ...

Midnight blue eyes.

Her heart did the strangest thing—it was as if the organ did a little flip when their gazes met. Such an unusual reaction, especially since she had only seen him once before and then never again after that.

Not that she had been hoping to see him all this time.

Liar, came a whisper from her head.

"You're not alone," Willa stated, shutting the voice away.

Queen Sybil flashed her a sheepish grin. "Yes, I meant to tell you. I would have messaged you, but you don't have a cell phone."

Her grip on the doorknob tightened. "Wh-what do you want?"

It was the king who spoke first. "Willa, I'm so sorry to disturb you so late at night, but we come here on urgent business. I'll get straight to the point. Do you remember Thoralf?"

She could barely meet those midnight blue orbs as she nodded.

"He's been away for two years now, seeking the solution to our problem."

"O-our p-problem?"

"The Wand, my lady." His voice was just as she remembered. Rich and smooth, like hot chocolate on a cold day. But the words he spoke left her chilled. "I have traveled all over the world looking for a solution and finally ... this is the closest I have come to any information on how to reverse The Wand's effects." He reached into the rucksack in his left hand and pulled out an old book. "Can you read this?"

Willa squinted at the cover. "I ... old runes ..." The etchings on the leather were faded, but she did recognize them. "Those are the old writings. But how? I thought only my clan used them."

The Dragon Guard looked relieved. "Then I was right. Which means you'll be able to translate what's in this book and help us find the location of the temple."

She glanced at the book warily. "A temple?"

"Yes. An ancient temple in Fiorska. The previous ... owner of the book said the cure was there. A cure that could reverse the effects of The Wand."

Willa slammed the door shut so hard her ears rang.

No!

She did not want to hear this.

I'm happy now. I don't want to go through that again.

I can't go back there.

I can't hope ...

"Willa?" came Queen Sybil's voice. "Please, talk to us."

Willa twisted the knob in her hand and jerked it open. "Talk to you?" she spat. "Why would I talk to you? I didn't even know you were searching for a cure."

"Hear us out," the queen pleaded. "We did not tell you because ... I thought it best. You seemed to be coming out of your shell once we started spending time together and I didn't know if speaking about The Wand would trigger you."

"I ... was unsure if I would even find a cure," Thoralf stuttered. "But I had to try anyway, because it's my fault King Harald lost his dragon. My honor is on the line."

King Harald ... oh, how could she forget? The former king had been hit by The Wand too. *So, that's why he set out on finding the cure*, she thought bitterly. Well, why did she think he did it? For *her*? "I suppose if you did find a cure to

The Wand's effects, then you'd want to use it on your former king?"

"Of course," he answered.

"And what about me? Will I get my dragon back? Can you guarantee it?"

"I—" Thoralf's mouth shut closed.

"Given a choice, you'd restore your king's dragon first, right? For your honor?"

His blond eyebrows snapped together. "My lady, it's not that simple. Besides, we won't know what the cure is until we read what is in that book."

"And you need me to translate it," she stated. "And to lead you to the temple on Fiorska."

"Yes, we need you."

She looked at Queen Sybil. "And if I don't want to? Will you force me to do it? Banish me if I don't?"

"Of course not," she replied quickly. "I promise you, we won't. You're my friend, Willa, I wouldn't do that to you. But tell me, why wouldn't you even want to try?"

She gritted her teeth. "Tell me, if your entire family and all your friends and everyone you know were murdered right in front of you, would you go back to the scene of the crime? Would you want to relive those moments by returning to the one place where you lost everything?"

"I'm so sorry," Queen Sybil reached out to her, but she flinched away. "You're allowed to feel how you feel. But, please, don't say no right away. We will give you as much time as you need to think about it."

"Don't hold your breath," she spat, then slammed the door shut. Spinning on her heel, she marched to her bedroom and sat down on her bed, arms wrapping around herself.

Father …

The grief felt fresh as ever, the pain in her chest just as sharp. She'd learned to ignore it in the past two years, to push the memories away.

How dare they come in here and bring them back?

Her hands balled into fists as she punched them into the mattress, biting her lips to keep from raging.

I don't want to remember. I want to forget.

She was happy and content in her new life.

Hoping would only send her back to square one.

In those early days, she did allow herself to hope for a cure. That once again she would feel the presence of her animal within her. That she could take to the skies in her dragon form.

But as the days and weeks and months dragged on, no one could give her any answers or solutions. King Aleksei and the others only looked at her with pity. And so, she grew even more depressed, wanting to end it all.

Yes, it was cowardly of her. And perhaps selfish. The main reason she couldn't go on was that she felt like nothing. That she was nothing without her dragon.

But she'd made peace with that now. Content to live her days quietly, away from others. She didn't want to have her hopes lifted, only to send them crashing again.

Willa gritted her teeth. The Wand was safe. Stored in a secret place on the Northern Isles and would never harm anyone else. That should be enough. It was time to put away hopes for any kind of cure.

CHAPTER 3

"That went about as well as I expected," Niklas drawled.

"Why did you not tell me there was another female dragon in the Northern Isles?" Annika admonished. "Why do you keep her a secret?"

"She's not exactly a secret," Queen Sybil said. "But Willa is sensitive. It took me months of trying to befriend her before she let me in."

"And even before Sybil came, she refused to speak with anyone," King Aleksei added.

They had told everyone a brief version of what happened to the Ice Dragons and Lady Willa on the way to the cottage. Hearing it all over again brought sadness to Thoralf, so he could sympathize as to why Willa wouldn't want to relive the past by going back to her former home.

When he first laid eyes on her moments ago, he was tongue-tied, unable to speak at how stunning she looked. Perhaps it was just that he hadn't seen her in years, he told himself. He also noticed the change in her. Yes, she was as beautiful as ever, but the anger was gone.

Then when he mentioned Fiorska and going back, he saw the same look in her eyes he did two years ago. The sadness, rage, and fear creeping in like shadows as night fell. He could not blame her if she didn't want to go back there.

But she was the key to finishing his quest and restoring his honor. The cure was at their fingertips, yet so far.

"Let's head back to the palace, and you can tell us more about this book," Aleksei said. "Perhaps we can find another way to unlock its secrets."

Soon, they gathered in the king and queen's private apartments, and after Queen Sybil called for coffee and refreshments, they sat down in the living room to reconvene.

"What can you tell us about the book and this cure?" King Aleksei began. "How did you even find it?"

"It all started when the second wand came into play," Thoralf said. A few months ago, the king and queen had been attacked while visiting Venice, and they discovered the Knights had obtained a second wand that had similar powers to the original one, albeit it only temporarily disabled a shifter's animal. "Gideon and Ginny were able to find more information about it, which led me back to a seafaring tribe in the Jorea region in the Caribbean."

"It was pure luck," Ginny interjected. "The Agency had a few operations there and had encountered that nomadic tribe of sea creature shifters." Ginny worked as an agent for The Shifter Protection Agency, a secret organization that protected shifters from those who sought to harm them, like the Knights of Aristaeum.

"They were quite difficult to track down," Thoralf

mentioned. "But I did find them, and their leader told me about the book. You see, according to their leader, the book was given to them a long time ago by a dragon who visited their tribe. Apparently, the dragon had been lost and turned around during a hurricane and sought shelter with them. He stayed for a few months, and the book was one of his possessions. The dragon didn't have much else, so he would tell them stories from the book. Eventually, the dragon went back to his home, but he left the book with them for safekeeping. No one knew how to read the words in the book, but everyone had heard the stories numerous times and they passed them from generation to generation."

"Like stories living on through oral tradition," Annika said.

"Exactly," Thoralf said. "They told me the stories, and one of them sounded like they were talking about the wizard, Aristaeum and The Wand." He took a deep breath. "The stories even spoke about the second wand—that it might actually have been the first attempt of creating The Wand, which is why its effects were only temporary."

"Makes sense," Rorik said, stroking his ruddy beard with his fingers. "What else did you learn?"

"That there may be a cure to The Wand's effects. The story goes on to say that one of Aristaeum's rivals, Ephyselle, created an antidote to The Wand. She made it in secret in her temple, which was located on the edge of the world, and hid it there."

"That's what the Ice Dragons call their home, Fiorska," King Aleksei said.

"Exactly." Thoralf flexed his hands, then brought them together. "From the other details in the stories, my guess is,

Ephyselle was part of the Ice Dragon clan or at least lived among them. And that this book was a spell or potion recipe book, as well as a diary where she wrote about Aristaeum and how she had planned to thwart him. I asked to see this book and when I saw the runes on the cover, I knew it had to have originated from the Ice Dragons and the dragon who had brought it to them in the first place was one of them."

"You recognized the runes?" the queen asked. "How?"

Thoralf met Aleksei's gaze, as well as the rest of his friends. A look passed between the king and queen, and he guessed they were speaking privately through their mind link. Being Aleksei's mate, Thoralf didn't mind if the king told Queen Sybil about his origins, but now wasn't the place or time.

The queen cleared her throat. "Apologies, Thoralf. Please, go on."

"No apologies needed, Your Majesty." He turned back to the others. "I asked if I could borrow the book, and he was happy to give it to me."

"He just gave you this hundreds-of-years-old artifact?" Gideon asked, his tone incredulous.

"Yes. See, the tribe doesn't believe in keeping material possessions, and because a dragon had brought them the book, he was happy to give it back to our kind."

"Do the oral stories give more information about this supposed cure?" Niklas asked. "Isn't there any way we could make it ourselves?"

"Nothing conclusive or solid, I'm afraid. In fact, it sounded like the story didn't have any kind of ending." Thoralf took the book out from the bag and opened it to the last page, where writings stopped in the middle. "I think whoever wrote this book didn't have time to finish it. Perhaps something happened to him or her."

"It could be the Ice Dragon who left it with the tribe did so deliberately, so as to hide the book's existence from Aristaeum," Ginny concluded, then snapped her fingers. "Can't we go to Fiorska and search for this temple? Surely with the right equipment we could eventually find it."

"The Ice Dragon's territory covers nearly the entire Greenland," King Aleksei pointed out. "It could take months or even years, plus, we need Lady Willa's permission to go there. She still technically holds that territory, being her father's heir. I suppose we could petition the Dragon Council to strip her of the title so that we may be free to go there."

"Like they did with my ancestors?" Queen Sybil scoffed. "Nuh-uh. No way."

"Perhaps we could find a way to translate the book ourself," Annika offered. "Like my father's diaries."

"We could try," Gideon said. "But it's going to take a while since we don't have any reference material to start with. Surely the Ice Dragons have some kind of library or information center."

"But that would mean having to step foot in Fiorska," Rorik pointed out. "Which brings us back to the same problem." He sighed. "If only we could find someone to translate it."

"We do. She's already here." *If things had been different, there would have been* another *other way.* Thoralf shook his head. The past was past, and there was no way to change it now. "I must talk to her," he said. "Convince her to help us."

Queen Sybil shook her head. "Not tonight. She's living

through the trauma again, and we don't want to push her away."

"Can't you talk some sense into her, Your Majesty?" Lady Vera asked. "Surely she will listen to reason."

"Her trauma runs deep," Stein said, placing an arm around his mate. "We must give her time."

King Aleksei rested his chin on his knuckles as his eyebrows furrowed together. "There is nothing more we can accomplish tonight, I'm afraid. You should all go back and get rest, you especially, Rorik. Do not keep your bride waiting too long." He sat up straight. "Perhaps after a good night's sleep, we can come up with some kind of plan to translate the book."

Everyone stood up and said their goodnights, but Thoralf stayed behind. Once they were alone, he turned to Aleksei. "I swear to you, I will not give up. We are so close."

The king grinned at him. "I know you won't. You never do."

"I just don't know how to proceed." Thoralf frowned. "How can we can convince Lady Willa to help us?"

"We need to get her to trust us," Queen Sybil said with a sigh. "I see that now. Though I've spent a lot of time with her, she's never opened to me about her past. I thought I was being respectful, but she's obviously bottling a lot inside."

Thoralf thought for a moment. "How did you initially befriend her? You sent her dozens and dozens of letters and invitations, and they all went unanswered." He remembered how Queen Sybil would send Lady Willa handwritten notes, inviting her to dinner or tea at the palace. At one point, Thoralf himself delivered the wedding invitation to the cottage, but it seemed Lady Willa hadn't even been there.

He'd been disappointed as he had hoped to see a glimpse of her before he left, as he'd already decided to go on his quest.

The queen chuckled. "It wasn't easy. I basically barged my way in and didn't give her a choice." Her eyes sparkled. "I wish I had known what she was like before all this. I bet she was one of those strong, stubborn girls that you couldn't give up on. In fact, you need to keep on pressing and chipping away, because the moment you back off, those walls are going to go up again. She kinda reminds me of a good friend of mine, whose mate basically had to bully her into being with him."

"I don't think we can bully Willa," Aleksei pointed out.

"That's not what I meant, darling." She patted him on the hand. "We can't give up on her. I won't. But we can't treat her like an invalid who's going to break at any moment either. She's a lot stronger than you all give her credit for. Now," she turned to Thoralf. "You must be exhausted. As you know, we always have a guest room ready in the palace. Please, stay there for as long as you like."

King Aleksei beamed at him, "And now that you're back with us, my friend, we should talk about your future."

"Thank you, Your Majesties, but my quest isn't over yet. Not until I've restored the king's dragon." Which meant he wasn't officially back with the Dragon Guard. "But I will accept your hospitality. I know where the guest rooms are and will take my leave." He placed his hand over his heart and bowed deeply before leaving.

As he made his way out, Thoralf pondered on the queen's words about Lady Willa. He agreed that she was strong—after all, she had gone through so much strife in such a short period of time. But at the same time, it was because of what had happened that everyone around her walked on eggshells, afraid to set her off.

But perhaps the queen was right. While Thoralf may not know much about women, he did know a lot about persevering and never giving up.

It may seem like a Sisyphean task to get Lady Willa on their side, but he couldn't give up now. *Not when I've gone through so much and come so far.*

Despite the long journey back, Thoralf couldn't sleep a wink. Normally he found it easy to bed down just about anywhere. However, not even the luxurious sheets and plush mattress underneath him could lull him into sleep.

Perhaps I'm not used to such opulent surroundings.

His last bed was soft shores by the ocean, after all.

Or perhaps there was another reason.

Each time he closed his eyes, the image of sad ice blue eyes and that beautiful face appeared in his mind.

If he were honest with himself, this was not the first time this had happened. Since he left the Northern Isles, something would remind him of her—the ice caps in Alaska or spying a blonde-haired woman crossing the street from the corner of his eye—and his mind would inevitably drift to Lady Willa. Of course, it was just a passing thought, and he would immediately dismiss it.

Thoralf rolled over and swung his legs over the side of the bed. Being a shifter, he didn't require as much sleep as humans did and was not tired. But still his brain remained active. Maybe a good flight would help him clear his thoughts and relax his mind.

The sky was still dark when he stepped out of the guest room balcony. Leaping off the edge, he quickly shifted into his dragon form and took to the skies. Despite having done this a million times, that initial rush of flying through the air never ceased to amaze him. Such a wonderful and unique feeling, something he would never take for granted, especially considering what could have happened.

Thinking back to that fateful day never failed to darken his and his dragon's moods. Shame, grief, and anger poured through him at his failure to protect his king and the only father figure he had ever known. It was the one thing he promised to do, and he had failed.

But he was so close to restoring his honor and his king's dragon. The solution was right here.

Thoralf blinked as he noticed the sky growing pink in the horizon. How long had he been flying? And more importantly—where had his dragon taken them?

Where are we?

The animal, of course, didn't answer, at least not with words. However, when Thoralf spied the familiar-looking cottage in the distance, he knew exactly where they were. A feeling of warmth spread through him as memories from long ago surfaced. Such a happy place, this cottage ...

The animal sped up toward the cottage, then landed just outside. Thoralf Cloaked himself immediately.

Why in the world did you bring us here?

The dragon only answered with a snort.

Before Thoralf could even contemplate his animal's strange behavior, a creaking sound made him freeze. Sure enough, the cottage's door opened, and Lady Willa stepped out.

Thoralf held his breath. Bathed in the rays of the rising sun, her skin seemed to glow. Her light, silvery locks were bound in a loose braid that draped over her shoulder. Even dressed simply in a robe, she seemed regal as a queen, and more beautiful than ever.

Thoralf had met many gorgeous women in his lifetime. He'd traveled the world, and before that, had escorted Aleksei when he went to college in Oxford. He'd even felt attraction to some of them, though he never acted on it.

But what he felt right now seemed so much more than attraction. It eclipsed every other feeling he'd ever had for a woman. It made him dizzy, and he momentarily lost his balance causing him to step back. The sharp snap of a branch that connected with the bottom of his booted foot made him cringe.

Lady Willa turned in his direction and inhaled a sharp breath. "If you're coming to spy on me, at least do a better job."

Shame filled Thoralf, and he Uncloaked himself. "Forgive me, Lady Willa. I was not spying on you."

A light blonde eyebrow lifted. "Then what are you doing here?"

He scrambled for an answer. "To watch the sunrise." He nodded at the horizon overlooking the edge of the cliff. "This part of the island always had the best views."

She pursed her lips but said nothing and instead turned toward the sea.

Silence stretched on between them, and the sun continued to ascend until the last traces of dawn disappeared and the sky was filled with the bright light of morning.

She turned her head toward him. "How long are you planning to stay there?"

Thoralf answered without missing a beat. "As long as it takes."

They stared at each other as he waited for a reaction, but her face remained blank. Disappointment filled him that she didn't remember the words he had spoken to her all those years ago. But then again, she had been recovering from a life-threatening injury and suffered a humungous loss, so he couldn't blame her if she didn't recall what he said.

"Do you like the sunset too, Lady Willa?" he said, breaking the tension.

"Yes," she answered, then wrinkled her nose. "How did you know?"

"Fiorska has six months of daylight and six months of darkness," he stated. "It must be a marvel for you to see both in the same day, every day."

A flash of surprise crossed her face but was quickly replaced by an indifferent mask.

A brief feeling of triumph surged through Thoralf, because for just a moment, he felt as if he'd chipped away at a tiny piece of that wall surrounding Lady Willa of the Ice Dragons. "I, too, enjoy the sunset," he stated. "You know, this cliff also has a good view." He gestured westward. "Perhaps I'll see you later this evening."

Before she could answer, he turned on his heel and walked away. Smiling to himself, he shoved his hands into his pockets.

It had taken the queen months before Lady Willa

allowed her past her walls. *I don't have that luxury.* He'd already wasted too much time searching for clues and going on wild goose chases. Besides, who knows what the Knights were up to and when they would strike next? *I must find that cure now.* One way or another, he would get Lady Willa on their side and help with translating the book.

Failure was not an option.

CHAPTER 4

Willa told herself she was not looking forward to sunset.

Absolutely, positively not.

Still, the entire day, she kept looking outside her window, her heart leaping at every little sound or shadow. Being that it was the height of summer, sunset came much later than it usually did. While she usually loved the longer daylight hours, today the sunshine tortured her with its presence.

She let out a frustrated sound and placed the plate she had been washing back into the water-filled sink. She'd just finished a late supper and was now cleaning up, though she had scrubbed that same plate over and over again. Her mind kept drifting off as she stood in front of the sink.

As long as it takes.

Sometimes Willa wondered if it had all been a dream—that she had conjured up the handsome Dragon Guard in her delirious state. After all, she'd never seen him again after that day. From time to time, she'd wonder. But the image of midnight blue eyes never faded from her memory, clear as the day she saw them.

Even if he comes, I should ignore him.

Willa blew out a breath. That's what she should do. But there was something about him that piqued her curiosity. If she still believed in the Goddess, she would have believed they somehow had some cosmic connection. What was it about him that she was drawn to?

Well, there was the fact that he was handsome. But Willa was no stranger to handsome men. In fact, as daughter of the Alpha, plenty of good-looking men in their clan paid attention to her. She'd even had a few relationships here and there, both casual and committed, though none lasted very long.

It had been too long since she'd been with a man. Maybe she was just feeling ... lonely, and he was the first unattached male she'd seen in a long while. And he was coming back tonight, right? To see her?

Or maybe it was just to convince her to help him with that book.

Willa bit her lip. Perhaps she'd overreacted, but there was no way she was going back there. Why couldn't they just leave it be? If she'd learned to live without her dragon, then so could Prince Harald.

Glancing toward the kitchen window, she saw that the sky was beginning to darken at the edges. Quickly, she finished up her washing and left the dishes to dry, then removed her apron before hanging it on the hook by the kitchen doorway. She smoothed her hands down her long, loose hair and straightened her blouse before stepping outside.

"I'm glad you decided to come out."

The low bass of Thoralf's voice caressed her skin, making her shiver despite the warm evening air. She turned her head toward him and noticed that he had changed into crisp, new clothes. Though the design was the same white linen shirt and trousers that he wore last night, those had been threadbare and yellowed. The ones he donned now were obviously newer. He did say he'd been traveling all this time, so it made sense that his clothes would be worn. Her nose wrinkled, however, when she noticed how scruffy his beard was and that his hair was growing long. She'd rather liked his clean-cut and shaven look from that first time she saw him.

"Is there anything the matter, my lady?"

She shook her head. "No." Turning away, she walked toward the edge of the cliff, and he followed her.

"This really is one of the best locations on the island," Thoralf began as he stopped right beside her. "Located right on the northern tip with unobstructed views. You could stand at this spot and watch the sun rise from the east and then sink down into the west." He chuckled. "It's also a great place to dive into the ocean, if you're feeling adventurous."

Willa peered over the edge of the cliff, down to the churning waters below. "Very adventurous." She furrowed her brows. "You seem to know a lot about this place."

"Of course, my lady." He nodded back to the cottage. "I used to live here."

Her jaw nearly unhinged. "Th-this place belongs to you?" He owned her home?

He shook his head. "No, no, I do not own it. The king does."

"I don't understand."

The corners of his mouth turned up. "He allowed my

parents to live in this cottage. I was born here." Turning toward her, he fixed those midnight blue eyes on her. "It's fitting that you are here now."

"Fitting? How?"

"Yes." His intense stare sent a strange sensation up and down her spine. "Do you feel this connection to me? Like I do with you?"

Her heart thudded madly. "A connection?"

"Lady Willa, my mother was one of your kind. An Ice Dragon."

Shock seared through her veins, and for a moment, her brain disconnected from her body. "You are half Ice Dragon?"

He nodded. "Her name was Isadura."

"My father never told me about the existence of another female Ice Dragon." As far as she knew, she was the only female Ice Dragon born in the last two decades.

"I'm afraid the Ice Dragons were not very happy that she decided to leave your clan for a Water Dragon," he began. "Back then, there were more of you—us dragons in general—and the Ice Dragons actually had a military outpost on the southern part of your territory. She lived there with her unit and met my father during some cooperative exercises with the Northern Isles' Royal Dragon Navy."

Willa searched her brain. "Yes, I remember now. I overheard some of our senior members talking about the outpost." Apparently, with their numbers dwindling, there really had been no need to keep it open, so the clan decided to close it and have everyone live in the main compound.

"She met my father and became pregnant with me, but didn't tell him right away. The Ice Dragons were overjoyed that she was with child, of course, but then she told them there was a possibility I'd be a Water Dragon. They didn't like that at all."

Willa understood as Ice Dragons were proud but also preferred to stick to their own kind. But it also made her cringe, thinking about how they would have treated Isadura and her unborn child. "I'm sorry."

"It's not your fault." His smile turned wistful. "So, she left and came here, then found my father. He was thrilled with the news, as was King Harald. He let them live in this cottage, and I was born here. Sadly, my father died shortly after that in the line of duty. Then my mother died of a mysterious illness when I was five."

"I'm so sorry." Contrary to popular belief, shifters were not immortal, nor were they impervious to sickness. They healed quickly from wounds, but there were a few illnesses that could affect or even kill them. "What happened after?"

"The king adopted me as his ward, and I went to live at the palace," he said. "But still ... this place brings back a lot of memories."

"You still remember her? Your mother, I mean?"

"I do. Well, bits and pieces. But what does remain in my memory is quite vivid. In fact, that's how I recognize the runes in the book. She had this pendant that had the same writings. I'm afraid I was too young to learn the language before she passed."

That damned book again!

Willa balled her hands into fists at her sides. "I told you, I'm not going to translate that book, nor am I going back there! If that's why you're here, then you've wasted your time."

Of course that's why he was here. Why else? Did she think he was here for *her*?

She spun away from him and was about to march back to the cottage—*his cottage, apparently*—when she felt a gentle hand on her arm. The shock of their bare skin touching made her stop.

"My apologies. Please, don't be angry with me." He released a slow breath. "I only want to fulfill my duty as a Dragon Guard and restore my honor."

She closed her eyes. His plea was so sincere and pure that her resentment melted away. It was difficult to be angry at him, not when she understood all about duty and honor.

"I know you want to do right by your king," she began. "B-but I can't ... go back there. Don't you understand?" It was too much. Even if they demolished the compound and removed all traces of the bloodshed, her heart would always remember the place where her entire world had been ripped from her.

"Perhaps you won't have to," he said. "Maybe the answers lie in the book. And all you have to do is translate it for us and give us permission to go there."

"And when you find the cure? Who will you give it to? Surely your king and I are not the only ones the Knights used The Wand on. What about us? Who gets to fight for us and the injustice done to us?"

He was silent for a moment. "My lady, I do not even know if the cure exists. It could be this book is pure fiction. But I must try. And you are right."

Right? "About what?"

"About everyone whose animals were taken away by The Wand. It would be selfish and unjust for us to keep the cure for only our king. So, I promise, if we do find such a cure, surely, we can find a way to replicate it so that everyone affected by The Wand can have their animals restored. That is the *right* thing to do."

She stared at him, unmoving and not speaking for what felt like forever. How could she reply to such a statement?

As her father's only child, she knew that someday she'd be Alpha and thus, her father raised her to be a leader, to know the importance of duty and honor and serving their people. Being Alpha wasn't just about being the head of the clan. There were responsibilities and burdens, and sometimes that meant she may have to do things that she didn't want to.

Even if it's difficult, my treasure, you must always strive to do the right thing.

Her father's voice rang in her ears, clear as a bell as if he'd been right there, whispering in her ear.

"All right."

Surprise registered on his face. "My lady?"

"I'll help you translate the book. If you promise we will find a way to restore *everyone's* animals. Not just your king's, and not just mine, but we must find anyone still alive that had been touched by that ... vile thing and help them too."

He bowed his head. "You have my word as a Dragon Guard of the Northern Isles."

She crossed her arms over her chest. "Bring the book to me tomorrow, and I will start."

"Thank you, my lady."

The sun had finished setting long ago, and now, they were surrounded by darkness. "It's growing late," she stated.

"Then I will take my leave. I shall come at half past nine so as not to disturb you too early."

Willa bit her lip as she nearly told him that he wasn't a bother. "All right."

"Thank you, Lady Willa." Turning on his heel, he walked away from the cottage, disappearing into the line of trees just at the end of the property.

Willa watched him, rooted to the spot until she heard the familiar flap of wings, though she didn't see his dragon. Strange that he would Cloak himself before flying off. This was the Northern Isles, after all, and seeing dragons was not an unusual thing.

A thought popped into her head. Did he do that for her? So that she would not have to see his dragon and remember her own lack of it?

She huffed. Such an unnecessary gesture. But she appreciated his thoughtfulness. If she were being honest, she was more disappointed that he had left so quickly.

He's only been back one day, she reminded herself. Maybe he was tired and needed to adjust to the time difference. Or visit friends he hadn't seen in a while. Or perhaps a lover ...

Her stomach knotted at such a thought. It wasn't her concern or business who he slept with, after all. Still, she couldn't help but feel disturbed at her own reaction. However, there were more important things to ponder on. Like, why did she agree to help them?

It wouldn't just be helping them.

Willa squashed the thrill in her veins at the thought of getting her dragon back. It might all be a wild goose chase, after all. The book could tell them nothing.

Or it could tell us everything.

Besides, if there was even a chance that they could help other people like her, then they needed to take it. It's what her father would have done. It was the right thing to do.

For the first time in a very long time, she allowed herself to hope.

CHAPTER 5

Thoralf's dragon became uneasy as they flew away from the cottage.

I know you miss this place, he told his dragon. *But it's no longer ours.*

Though Isadura left him so suddenly and tragically, Thoralf only had happy memories of living in that cottage with her. Laughing, playing, and when it was time for him to learn to shift into his dragon, she'd been the one who helped and encouraged him and taught him how to work with his animal. He'd never felt more safe and loved.

Spying the palace in the distance, he guided his dragon to the front lawn and landed on his human feet with a soft thud.

Aleksei, he called. *Apologies for disturbing you so late, but I must speak with you. And Prince Harald as well.* His heart hammered in his chest at the thought of facing the former king. He'd not seen nor spoken with the prince all this time.

Of course, Aleksei replied. *Fortunately for you, I am with him now in my office, having a late meeting. We shall be waiting.*

Thoralf pushed aside the urge to flee, so he wouldn't have to face Prince Harald and be reminded of his failure. But he had no choice. Hopefully, he would not disappoint him for a second time.

He quickly made his way to the west wing, where the palace's business offices were located. His palms were sweaty by the time he walked into Aleksei's private office.

"Your Majesty, Your Highness," he greeted, bowing his head deeply. "Thank you for—"

"Thoralf!" Prince Harald greeted as he rose from his chair and strode over to him. "You are here. Why did you not tell me?"

He lifted his head slowly, bracing himself for the look of disappointment on Prince Harald's face. To his surprise, the prince greeted him with a warm smile and a firm grip on his shoulders. "It has been too long, Thoralf. I'm so glad to see you safe."

Thoralf swallowed to relieve the burning sensation in his throat. "Forgive me, Your Highness."

"For not coming to see me right away? Of course, you are forgiven." He drew Thoralf in for a hug. "And for the past ... never. Because there is nothing to forgive. I told you that. It was not your fault."

Thoralf breathed a sigh. He did not believe that, of course, but hearing it from the prince mollified him. Clearing his throat, he pulled away. "You are looking fine and healthy, Your Highness."

"I have spent the afternoon with my dear Alric," the prince said proudly. "Nothing makes me feel younger that being with him. He is so handsome and strong."

Aleksei gestured to the empty chair by his desk. "Please, why don't we sit down and you can tell us your news."

He waited for the prince to take his seat and opted to remain standing. "I'll be brief." He told them of his conversation with Lady Willa.

"She truly will help us?" Aleksei asked. "I don't know what you said to her, but I'm glad you were able to change her mind."

Thoralf chewed at his lip. "Prince Harald, I probably should have consulted you before I struck that bargain with Lady Willa. I know you have been waiting a long time to have your dragon restored."

Prince Harald stood up to face him. "I must admit, in the following weeks after I had my dragon taken away, I wallowed in grief. The emptiness ... the silence ... it nearly drove me mad." He blew out a heavy breath. "Which is why I wouldn't wish it on anyone else. My boy, I am happy to wait a while longer if it means we can help everyone affected by The Wand. You did the right thing."

"Your Highness ..." The thickness in his throat prevented him from saying anything else, but from the way the prince beamed at him, he knew there was no need for more words.

"It's settled then," Aleksei interrupted, breaking the tension in the air. "You must assist Lady Willa in any way you can, provide her with what she needs to do the translation work. Work with her closely until you finish."

"As you wish, Your Majesty." Thoralf wouldn't question his king's orders after all.

"Now," Prince Harald motioned to the chair in front of him. "Why don't you sit down for a moment? I'd love to hear more about your travels."

Thoralf was only too happy to oblige, after all, he hadn't seen the prince in almost two years. Prince Harald wanted to know about all the places he visited and the people he met, and so he regaled them with the best stories from his journey.

"Oh my," Prince Harald said with a loud yawn as he glanced at the clock. "I didn't even realize how late it is."

"Sybil is looking for me." Aleksei got to his feet and stretched his arms out. "I must head back."

"So must I," Prince Harald added. "Come, let us retire for the evening. You have much work ahead of you, and you need rest."

"Thank you, Your Highness." How he would be able to rest tonight, he wasn't sure. His dragon, too, felt anxious and excited.

I know how you feel, he told his animal. Tomorrow could be the start of the end of his crusade.

Thoralf showed up at the cottage at exactly half past nine. "Good morning, Lady Willa," he greeted when she opened the door. His heart stuttered at her loveliness. Today, her hair was pinned up in a bun on top of her head, while a few stray tendrils added some softness to the angular lines of her face. She wore a simple pair of trousers and a linen top.

"You're on time," she noted.

"Of course." He could sense the irritation in her tone. "I'm sorry, is it still too early? Should I wait until later—"

"No—I mean ..." She blew out a breath, sending a lock of stray hair flying. "I lost power this morning and so I couldn't have a proper cup of tea. I think it's the solar panels, but I wouldn't know the first thing about fixing them."

"Did you not call the palace for help?"

She nodded. "The head of operations said they'd get to me as soon as they can, but they're backed up. They're sending a generator but not until later this evening."

"I shall take a look then."

"You don't—"

"It's fine." He handed her the book. "I can check for a loose connection or perhaps the panels themselves need to be replaced. If anything, I can fetch the generator for you now so you may have your tea."

"Th-thank you." She hugged the book to her chest. "I'll be inside."

Thoralf walked to the back of the cottage and found an old ladder in the shed. He proceeded to climb up to the roof where the solar panels were. They were all intact as far as he could tell, but he noticed the apple tree on the west side of the cottage was overgrown and its branches brushed the panels. Walking over, he found the problem—a disconnected line. One of the branches likely pulled the wires out that went into the battery. He reconnected it quickly. Using his keen hearing, he focused his ears and waited for the hum of the batteries charging up.

"There you go." He wiped his hands downs his trousers. Thankfully it was an easy fix, but it was bound to happen again unless the branch was trimmed back. *I should get someone to fix that.* The tree badly needed pruning too and might become a danger to the cottage and Lady Willa. Heading back down, he knocked on the door.

"Come in."

He poked his head through the doorway, but did not enter. "My lady, I have reconnected the solar panels to the battery, so do check in a few minutes if your power is back on. I must head out on an errand, but I'll be back soon."

He didn't wait for an answer in case she was busy, so he shifted into his dragon form. He flew back to the palace to search for the head gardener, Mr. Olsen James. When he got to the maintenance office, he was told that Mr. James had retired a few weeks ago and they were still searching for a replacement.

"If there's anything you need, you can fill out a request form," the harried-looking young man working alone in the office said. "But I don't know when we'd get to it. We have a few vital repairs in the pipeline."

"I see." He thought for a moment. "Perhaps I could do it myself. Do you have some equipment I could borrow?"

The young man gave him directions to the gardener's shed and told him to take what he needed. So, Thoralf found the shed and unearthed a pair of pruning shears and a new ladder before heading back to the cottage. To his surprise, Lady Willa emerged from the cottage the moment he reappeared.

"Where did you—" Her eyes landed on the shears and ladder. "What are those for?"

He quickly explained to her what happened. "And so I thought I would prune the tree myself."

"You don't have to do that."

"It won't take too long and will prevent this from happening again," he said. "Did the power come back on?"

Her face lit up. "It did, thank you. I'm enjoying my tea now."

"Good. Now, I should get to work."

"And so should I. Uh ... thank you."

"My pleasure, my lady." He gave her a nod and then walked toward the apple tree.

The job didn't seem too difficult or complicated at first, but the tree was quite massive, even bigger than Thoralf remembered. It looked like it hadn't been pruned in years, but he wasn't surprised. As far as he knew, no one had lived in the cottage since he left.

It was well past noon by the time Thoralf finished pruning the tree. The heat of the sun beat down on him so he had discarded his shirt long ago. When he was done, he examined his work.

"Not bad." The tree was now pruned back so none of the branches were touching the roof, but still provided shade for the bedroom. However, now that the overgrowth was cleared, he noticed that some of the roof shingles were broken. While the cottage itself was livable, time and neglect hadn't been kind to it. The paint on the shutters were peeling, the door sagged and creaked loudly, and the rose bushes had grown wild. An idea popped into his head, so he grabbed his discarded shirt, slung it over his shoulder, and strode back to the front door and knocked.

"I know it's you," Lady Willa said as she opened the door. "You don't have to knock each time—" She stopped short, her nostrils flaring and mouth clamping shut as her eyes traveled southward before they turned away into the distance.

"Apologies for disturbing you again." He glanced down and realized his naked chest was covered in sweat. *I must stink like a hog.* No wonder Lady Willa was speechless. "I have finished pruning the tree. Your solar panels should be safe."

"Th-thank you," she stammered, then met his gaze. "Work on the book has been slow, I'm afraid."

"Oh. Are they the wrong runes? Could it be it came from somewhere else?"

"No, it's not that. It's my fault. I mean, I know the runes, but haven't practiced reading them in years. We don't actually use them much anymore, not since we went digital a decade ago and we switched to Latin letters." Her teeth sank into her lower lip. "And I don't recognize some of them. They're probably very old. I could guess the meaning based on context, but it's taking me much longer than I thought."

"There is no rush, my lady," he said. "Take as much time as you need. And if you cannot do it, then we will find another way. Is there any way I could assist you? His Majesty said you can have whatever you need."

"Well, now that you mention it ..." She tapped a finger on her chin. "A computer with Internet access would be a good start. Maybe some writing materials? The only thing I have right now is the pen and notepad I use for my weekly grocery list. A couple of notebooks and office supplies will help me organize my notes and translations. Oh, and maybe even a scanner and printer."

"I can certainly get those things for you. But there is one thing I would like to ask."

"What is it?"

"If you would permit me, I would like to do some maintenance on the cottage."

She lifted a blonde eyebrow. "You make it sound like I'm doing you a favor."

"Well, in a way, yes. The outside of the cottage seems to have been left in disrepair—which is not your fault of course, but I'm worried for its structural integrity. I wouldn't want you to come to harm."

Her eyes grew wide. "Y-you wouldn't?"

"Of course, especially not when you are doing us a great service."

Her shoulders sagged. "Oh, of course."

"The door needs to be re-attached or even replaced. The shutters could use a fresh coat of paint, and I could clean up the garden so it's easier for you to maintain. Then I'll check the roof. I saw a few loose shingles when I checked on the solar panels. You might need new panels as well; I believe they're the same ones from when I was living here."

"You can do all that?" she asked, surprised.

"Everything except replace the solar panels," he chuckled. "Last year I spent a few weeks on a farm in Bolivia while I was waiting for a lead on The Wand. I helped the farmer and his wife, and they taught me a few things. Now, would that be amenable to you?"

"Of course."

"And it would be practical for me to be here, so if you need anything while you're working on the book, I'll be nearby," he pointed out. For some reason, this pleased his dragon, and if he were honest, himself as well. *Only because I want the book translated as soon as possible.*

"I suppose that makes sense. I was told Helgeskar Palace has a vast library; I might ask to borrow some books."

"I would be happy to fetch whatever you need, my lady."

"It's Willa," she said.

"I beg your pardon?"

"If you're going to be my handyman and helper, you can call me Willa."

"I don't—"

"Please."

He paused. "All right. Willa. And I'm—"

"Thoralf."

The way she said his name made something in his chest flare. "It's settled then. I shall go and source the equipment you need. If you don't mind, I shall take my leave."

"Wait! I mean ..." She blinked. "It's past lunchtime. Have you had anything to eat?"

"I'm afraid not, but I can find something in the kitchens."

"I have some food," she offered. "Just some cold sandwiches. You could join me. But of course, I'm sure the palace has much better—"

"I would love to join you," he said, a little too quickly. "I mean, if you don't mind sharing."

"Not at all." Stepping aside, she motioned for him to enter. "If you want to, uh, clean up, the bathroom's over there." She slapped a hand to her forehead. "Of course, you know where it is."

He flashed her a smile. "Thank you."

He marched to the bathroom, washed his hands and face in the sink, then dried himself as best as he could with the hand towel before putting his shirt back on. As he made his way to the kitchen, he couldn't help the wave of nostalgia coming over him. Most of the furniture had been replaced with brand new pieces, but he recognized the floral wallpaper in the living area, the comfy chair by the window, and the faded but clean carpet in the hallway. When he entered the kitchen, he swore he could hear his mother's laughter as she prepared dinner while he pestered her with all kinds of questions.

"Thoralf?"

Willa's voice jerked him back to the present. "Thank you for letting me wash up and for the food."

"It's the least I can do. After all, thanks to you, I didn't have to skip on my tea today." The corners of her mouth turned up slightly in an almost smile. "Please, sit. I was so engrossed in the book, I forgot to eat."

They sat down at the opposite ends of the table, and Willa poured him some cool water from a jug. "I don't get many visitors, so it's just meat, cheese and tomatoes. I do cook here and there, but it's been so warm lately, I just prefer cold lunches."

"I know what you mean." He took a sip of the cool water. "And the sandwiches look delicious, thank you."

"You haven't even tasted them yet." Her tone sounded teasing. "It could be the worst meal you've ever had."

"Oh, I've had some pretty terrible meals this past year, my la—I mean, Willa. Like, fermented seafood and boiled sheep parts." He took a bite of the sandwich, chewed, then swallowed. "This is miles away from that."

She looked visibly disturbed. "You ate fermented seafood and sheep innards? Why?"

"I could not be rude to my hosts." He took another bite. "My search didn't always take me to the nicest and fanciest cities. Oftentimes, I had to trek up mountains and rainforests. There were no five-star hotels or restaurants."

"I've never been anywhere else," she stated. "Well, once to Corum. It's an oasis in the desert."

"I have never been, but heard stories." The Sand Dragons' headquarters were said to be opulent and magnificent, a thriving city in the middle of the desert, said to be even older than the Northern Isles.

"Do you have a favorite place you've visited?" she asked.

"Ah, that is a difficult question to answer. Everywhere I went to had its own charm and appeal." He took a few more bites and finished the sandwich. "But I have to admit, one thing I can never forget about my travels is how kind and generous people could be." Indeed, he'd been surprised at the hospitality he experienced, especially from those who already had little to give. "Though, a few places do stand out."

She leaned forward as she put her sandwich down. "Which ones?"

"Off the top of my head ... the Taj Mahal in India, Machu Picchu in Peru, the Grand Canyon in America, and the temples of Cambodia."

"Such an exciting life you've led," she commented, then took a bite of her sandwich.

"Did you want to travel while you were growing up?"

Her brows furrowed. "I used to long to leave Fiorska when I was growing up. I hated how the seasons never changed." A dark look passed over her. "And now, I suppose, I got what I wished for."

The expression on her face caused a stabbing pain in Thoralf. "Forgive me, Willa. I did not mean to bring up the past."

"No, it's fine."

However, the tension in the room remained, and Thoralf desperately sought to break it. Standing up, he walked over to the back door that led out into the gardens. A shelf was propped up against the wall next to it, one he'd never seen before. He nudged it over a few inches to the right. "Ah, there it is."

"What is it?" Willa walked up behind him. "Did you find a spider or something?"

"Not at all." He pointed to the markings on the wall made with a pen with dates scribbled next to them. "My mother marked my growth on this very wall."

"Oh." Leaning down, she peered at the notches and ran a finger over them, stopping at the last one, when he turned five. "I never knew this was here."

"I can get some paint and cover it for you, if you like."

"No, no." She shook her head vehemently. "Don't do that. That might have been the last thing she wrote before she ..."

"Before she passed," he finished.

"It's a nice reminder. A memento of her."

"True, but I very well can't take this hunk of wall from the cottage."

"Of course not," she said. "But maybe you can take a picture. Or who knows?" She stood up straight. "Perhaps once we find the cure, I can leave the Northern Isles and you can have this cottage back. I'm sure it'll be a wonderful place to raise a family." Turning her back to him, she took the empty plates from the table and began to put them in the sink.

"Allow me—"

"No, I can do it."

While the earlier tension in the room had broken, the atmosphere hadn't returned to normal. Perhaps he'd overstayed his welcome. "Thank you for the meal, Willa. Now, if you'll excuse me, I shall head out and talk to Gideon about getting you the things you need. Is there anything else?"

"No, not at all." Her voice was tight, then her shoulders relaxed. Looking over her shoulder, she said, "Thank you for your help, Thoralf."

"Anytime, Willa. I'll see you tomorrow."

He made his way out quietly, so as not to disturb her. Once again, his dragon did not like them leaving, but he ignored it.

Thoralf wasn't sure what made her close up all of a sudden, especially since he'd thought they were having a nice chat. Perhaps she didn't want him to be overly friendly, and he had overstepped his bounds. But then, he remembered the queen's words about how Willa liked to build up walls around her. For some reason, he did not like the idea of her closing herself off from him like that.

Did it matter anyway? She'd already agreed to translate the book for them, and Aleksei and Prince Harald were onboard with the idea of finding a way to share the cure. Indeed, he didn't have to go back and do all the repairs on the cottage, much less befriend her. He could find someone else to do that as well as deliver all the equipment she needed.

But somehow, Thoralf found the thought of not seeing her every day unsettling. *And I promised her I would assist her*, he told himself. He certainly couldn't break his promise.

CHAPTER 6

Willa was upset. But the exact reason why confused her.

Sure, bringing up the past always hurt. Everyone and everything had been ripped from her all at once—her home, her family, her dragon. There was no way to process the grief and anger she felt when it happened as she was still recovering physically from her wounds. However, the grief had lessened over the years, but it would always be there. Over time, she had accepted this life without her family and her dragon and found some peace along the way.

Then he came along.

She had resisted the urge to hope, but somehow, Thoralf had wormed his way past her defenses. Sure, she was motivated by this small chance that they could restore her dragon, but more than that, she felt ... alive. Like her life had meaning and purpose once again. While she may not be Lady Willa, future Alpha of the Ice Dragons anymore, she had a chance to become something else.

So why was she upset at Thoralf again? Was it because he reminded her of the past, and caused her pain again?

Or maybe it was because he made her feel hope again. That she could have her dragon and move on with her life, but then, so could he. His quest would come at an end and then he would settle down and they would never have cause to see each other again.

Ridiculous.

She hardly knew him. Sure, she was attracted to him physically—that she could admit because she wasn't blind. When she'd seen him bare chested, she almost had a heart attack. To be honest, she had wondered what he looked like without his shirt, but seeing it in the flesh, so to speak, exceeded her expectations and imagination. That wide, muscled chest covered with tanned skin and glistening with sweat had her temperature rising a few degrees.

She sighed and finished washing the dishes, leaving them to dry on the rack. Trying to read that book was a monumental task, and she'd spent most of the morning leafing through it—and trying not to look out the window to watch Thoralf.

Her reading skills in the old language were rusty, but going through the book did help jog her memory. The language had roots in the old Viking runes, so if she could find something to compare them to, there might be a way to figure out their meaning.

But for now, she needed some rest, and there wasn't much she could do until Thoralf came back with the equipment she needed, so she spent the rest of the day cleaning up and reading.

The following day, Thoralf came back again at nine thirty on the dot.

"I have almost everything you need," he said, jerking his thumb back to the large crate behind him.

Her eyes widened. "You needed that huge box to carry a laptop and some paper?"

"I also brought you an office chair and table, plus a filing cabinet so you could set up a place to work."

He brought all of that for me? "You didn't have to."

"But I wanted to," he said with a grin. "Sitting down for hours will cause your muscles and joints pain, so I borrowed an ergonomic chair from one of the offices."

She didn't know what to say, so she let him inside so he could set up all the equipment he brought. They cleared a corner of the living area together so he could put the table and chair there.

"You should have everything you need," he said. "I need to go back to the palace and pick up the painting equipment so I can work on the shutters. I won't bother you anymore today, but do let me know if you need anything."

He didn't wait for her reply and quickly left. Once again, she felt upset by his hasty exit, but she quashed that ludicrous notion.

Shaking her head, she took the book and sat down at her new working desk. After setting up the laptop and labeling some folders for the file cabinet, she grabbed a fresh pad where she could jot down her notes as she read through the book, translating each rune she knew and leaving blank the ones she wasn't sure of.

Around noon, her stomach growled with hunger. Thoralf hadn't come back yet. She made herself sandwich and resisted the urge to make a second one just in case he came back soon and was hungry.

By the time she sat back down at her desk, she heard the sound of footsteps outside. The fluttering in her stomach told her it had to be Thoralf, but she calmed it down and concentrated on the book.

The rest of the afternoon passed without much incident, though Willa couldn't help but jump each time she heard a noise from the outside like the windows opening and shutting or the brushstrokes on wood. Still, she did her best to concentrate on translating what she could recognize from the book and writing them down on the pad, leaving space for the ones she couldn't recognize.

"Huh."

She read out the first lines she had translated. "Personal Diary of Ephyselle, Priestess of the Nightwing, Mate to Gustav, Alpha of the Ice Dragons."

The most peculiar feeling washed over Willa as she spoke the words. Like something stirred in her soul, telling her to continue. Her hands shook as she smoothed her palms across the page, and she silently read the rest of the paragraph.

Fiorska, Seventh Round of the Moon, Three Hundredth Cycle of Havarska

I am now finally confident of my writing skills to keep my own personal diary. My dearest Gustav has been so patient with me, teaching me how to write in his own language. I only hope to —— and that I can keep this record to share with our children and grandchildren someday.

My name is Ephyselle, Priestess of the Nightwing. Our tribe was visited by the winged men three cycles ago, as they came to aid us when the neighboring tribe of —— attacked. Though my tribe's magic was powerful, it was no match for our enemies and ——. We were on the brink of defeat when they came—beautiful, fierce creatures, crossing the skies. They saved our tribe from a terrible fate. Once the battle was over, we greeted our saviors. As it turned out, they were not creatures, but men who walked in animal skins.

To my surprise, their leader—"Alpha" as they called him—Gustav, declared me his mate as fated by the Goddess herself. In my soul and heart, I knew he was right, and so I came to live here, at the edge of the world, with him.

"Yes!" In her excitement, she shot up from the chair, making it tip over. It landed on the floor with a crash. "Oh no!"

A gust of wind rushed at her, and strong, warm hands engulfed her upper arms. "What's wrong? Are you hurt? Tell me."

She forced out a chuckle. "No, no! I'm fine."

He relaxed his grip but did not let go. "You sounded like you were distressed."

"Not at all." She peered up at his face. Had they ever been this close before? They were inches apart, and she could feel the warmth of his body. A furious blush crept up her neck and cheeks, and she stepped away from him. "I'm sorry for scaring you."

"But what is it? What made you cry out?"

She shrugged. "I ... it's silly really."

"Tell me."

"I translated a few lines successfully, that's all." She told him about what she'd discovered. "I mean ... there's nothing there about The Wand or a cure yet."

"But now we have proof that this book really did belong to a woman named Ephyselle," he pointed out. "And she calls herself a priestess. Perhaps that is what her tribe calls those who can use magic. From what I can remember from my history lessons, humans used to be able to wield magic."

"True." The Wand was proof of that, after all. Humans did once know how to use magic, but they somehow lost it over the centuries. "Still, this is only the first page."

"Do not discount your work, Willa," he said firmly. "Any effort you put forth brings us closer to the cure."

"But what if we're wrong? What if we waste all this time and it all turns out to be for nothing?" Was all this even worth it? The hours of work it might take, all the effort, and for what? She could end up being disappointed. She could disappoint *him*.

"If there's anything I've learned this past year, it is that any work I put into this quest isn't nothing. Was I dismayed each time a clue didn't pan out? Of course. But each dead end only eliminated a false clue, which only brought me closer to the truth."

It sounded so idealistic, yet she could not ignore the sincerity in his voice. Had she ever met anyone so pure? "I suppose you're right."

"I know I am." With a grin, he picked up her chair and placed it upright. "You are doing a wonderful job, Willa. I cannot thank you enough."

"Hopefully I can find some real information soon. Perhaps I should skip the first few pages? Surely, I don't need to know this woman's life story." However, something about that did not sit right with her. That now that she'd started Ephyselle's story, she had to know all of it.

"If you think that will help us. But, take your time. There is no need to rush the translation as we should aim for accuracy and not speed," he assured her. "Do you require anything else?"

"No, I'm fine for now."

"I am done painting the shutters," he declared. "I'll return tomorrow and work on the door then."

"Of course." She bit her lip, ignoring the disappointment tightening her chest. "I'll keep working on the diary."

"Do not overtire yourself," he warned. "Make sure you rest and have time for yourself. Otherwise, I will take the book away."

Was he teasing her? "I won't. But then you'll have to make sure I take a break by having lunch with me." *Oh dear*. What in the world made her say such bold worlds? "Assuming you don't mind, I mean."

His sensuous lips spread into a slow smile. "It would be no burden to sit down for a meal with you. Now, if you'll excuse me, I will take my leave." He gave her a respectful nod. "I shall see you then."

"See you." Her heart stuttered at the smile he flashed her. And she couldn't resist returning it with one of her own.

Willa wasn't sure how long she'd been standing there,

watching after him as he left, but it seemed like forever, and the fluttering butterflies in her stomach would not stop. And she found that she didn't want that feeling to end.

As he promised, the next day Thoralf joined her for lunch, which was a relief as Willa spent the entire morning fussing over the meal. She made some meat pies and salad, as well as some iced tea.

She attempted to work on the diary, but found that she couldn't sit still. When the familiar knock came, she nearly tipped the chair over again trying to get to the door. Her heart beat madly as his handsome, smiling face greeted her. Her gaze lowered, past his unkempt beard, to the golden skin displayed by the wide V of his half-opened shirt. *Oh dear*.

"Hello, Willa. Is your offer of lunch still good?"

"Of course." Quickly, she turned around, hoping he wouldn't notice her blush. "The pies are cooling, and they should be ready now."

They settled in, and she served the meal. Thankfully any awkward silence was filled with small talk, though mostly he did the talking as he spoke of his time growing up in the palace with Prince Aleksei.

"I had no idea you were practically brothers," she said. "Surely with such a connection, you could have done anything. Started your own business or maybe even become a minister."

He laughed as he finished off the last bit of crust from his pie. "Me, a minister? I don't think so. I've seen first-hand what politics are like; I even sat in Aleksei's classes in Oxford. No, thank you, I don't have the stomach for it."

"And you father's family?"

"He was the last of his house, sadly." A wistful look took over his face. "I would have been left to fend for myself if the king hadn't made me his ward. Though when that happened, I had to forsake his name."

"Oh."

"Do not be sad, Willa. I was very fortunate King Harald took me in. He and Aleksei treated me as if I was their own flesh and blood. I chose to become a Dragon Guard because I wanted to."

"That's lovely. And now I'm feeling ashamed of my clan," she said sheepishly.

"But why?"

She brushed a crumb off the table, unable to meet his gaze. "For how they treated your mother. You're still one of us, no matter who your father or your animal is. Unfortunately, Ice Dragons can be narrow-minded about things like blood and family. We prefer to keep to our own kind, and we only have humans around to serve us and for having children."

"That sounds ... harsh."

"They aren't slaves, kept against their will," she said defensively. "They are treated well and choose to be there."

"I didn't mean to imply such a thing, forgive me."

She gazed into his midnight blue eyes and saw only sincerity. "Of course. But I hope you let me explain."

"There's no need," he said. "But I am curious. No one knows much about the Ice Dragons."

"Like I said, we prefer to keep to ourselves." She poured

herself some tea and took a sip. "The edge of the world is a harsh place, but Ice Dragons prefer the cold and darkness. But in our human forms, we require more comfort, which is why we have our human staff. They are paid handsomely and may leave anytime. We recruit regularly from the outside world depending on our needs, but many of them have been with us for generations. It's the only life they've known. And besides that, if a human were to produce or sire a dragon child, they would be elevated to a higher status among our people, and they are taken care of for the rest of their lives. This ensures the survival of our clan."

"Of course. Dragonlings are rare and treasured."

"Exactly, and with Fiorska being such a harsh place, it's difficult for us to find people to live there. We support monogamy, of course. If two people want to be together, they simply decide on it, and they stay together for as long as they like. But sometimes that must be put aside for practicality."

"How so?"

"Once an Ice Dragon comes of age, they are encouraged to have children as soon as possible, even without any commitments or bonds." She paused, waiting for his reaction. However, he remained silent, his expression neutral. "To an outsider, such a thing sounds callous and unfeeling."

"Without context, yes," he replied. "But I've seen similar practices in my travels, especially among peoples whose numbers are dwindling. Indeed, your way sounds more pragmatic. And who am I to judge your practices, especially when it produces something as precious as a child?"

"But that's why I'm disappointed in my clan." She nearly lost her train of thought as she met his gaze once again. "Isadura should not have been tossed out like that. We should have accepted her and you." How would things have been different if Thoralf had grown up in Fiorska? Or if he'd been an Ice Dragon? She guessed he was a few years older than her. Perhaps when she had come of age, he would have courted her, and they could have become lovers.

"Shoulda, woulda, coulda."

She started. "I beg your pardon?"

"It's an expression I heard in America," he began. "Basically, it's an expression of regret over how things might have turned out. But we cannot change the past, only look to the future."

A warmth spread over her as Thoralf flashed her a hopeful smile, and she found herself returning it. "Shoulda, woulda, coulda," she repeated.

"This has been a wonderful meal, Willa," he said as he stood up. When she reached for a plate, he waved her away. "I will do the dishes. And I will not take no for an answer."

"I won't object then," she replied. "But I should get to work."

Over the next two days, Willa found herself in a routine that somehow incorporated Thoralf's presence. He always arrived at half past nine in the morning to check on her progress and fetch some books or other supplies for her. Then, by noon, he'd come in for some lunch, though their conversations remained light and casual, and Willa didn't offer more information about the Ice Dragons or about her past, nor did Thoralf ask.

After their meal, he'd work on the cottage while she continued her translation work. Though he finished the shutters, the door, and pruning the wild roses, he eventually found other tasks to do around the cottage and often stayed until mid-afternoon. Each time he left, Willa controlled the urge to invite him to stay for dinner; after all, she couldn't manipulate all his time, especially after he'd been gone for so long. Surely there were other people who wanted his company.

Like other women?

Groaning, she rested her head on top of the desk. The more time she spent with Thoralf, the more the attraction grew. She thought it would be the opposite—maybe she'd find he had a distasteful habit like chewing with his mouth open or he'd say something that would make him sound like an ass, but he was nothing but polite and charming.

Blowing out a breath, she lifted her head and went back to her translations. Frankly, reading Ephyselle's diaries had become the second-best part of her day, and she often worked well into the night so she could find out what happened next.

It was so eerie that she could be fascinated with this woman who existed hundreds of years ago. Like she could feel a connection to her even through the distance of time and space. Willa had attempted to skip ahead a few pages at first so she could get to the part of where the temple was located and find the cure, but it felt like there were missing pieces to the story, and she had to go back and find out what happened.

Fiorska, Fifteenth Round of the Moon, Three Hundredth and Second Cycle of Havarska

Today is the darkest day of my life. We have lost our beloved child.

"Oh." Her throat closed up as she read the most recent paragraph she had finished working on. A single teardrop fell on the notepad, smearing her handwriting. She bit the back of her hand, but she continued to read.

Gustav has been nothing but loving and supportive, despite his obvious disappointment. The healer said this was normal for women who conceived for the first time. She assured me that I am strong and healthy, and there will be another child, and I should not grieve.

But how can I explain to her that though I do believe that I could conceive and bring forth a child someday, it would not be this child we lost? That since I knew of its existence, I had been planning its future? And now that is all gone. All my hopes and dreams for this one being that existed for such a brief moment.

Willa couldn't help herself as the tears poured down her face and a sob broke from her throat. *Oh, Ephyselle.* Though she had never conceived herself, she felt the pain as if it were her own. She was so wrapped up in the grief that she didn't hear the door open.

"Willa, did you—"

Thoralf! Quickly, she wiped the tears from her face with her sleeves, but did not face him. "Yes?"

"What's wrong?" His footsteps pounded on the wood floor as he closed the distance between them. "What has upset you?"

"I-it's nothing." She sucked in a breath. "It's silly, really."

"Not if you're crying. Please." A careful hand landed on her shoulder, twisting her around to face him.

She forced a smile. "It's just this silly diary." When she lifted her head, the expression on his face was dead serious, so she told him about Ephyselle's loss. "Truly, Thoralf, it's just another story in the life a woman who's now dead and dust."

"What story?"

It was obvious he would not let this go, so she told him. "I'm always like this," she explained. "Even with the books I read. I always cry through the sad parts." However, she didn't quite feel the same way as she did now. Ephyselle had been a real person, after all. "Maybe ... maybe I should just skim through the book. Concentrate on finding references to a temple and Aristaeum and The Wand and translate those parts."

"No, don't do that." His voice was like a soft caress. "Surely, you must want to know Ephyselle's story and what happens to her?"

"What for? And what if it's more tragedy and grief? I should just skip over the sad parts."

"Never skip over the sad parts. They're a part of life, and in some ways, they give life more meaning and teach us that every moment is precious." He squeezed her shoulder. "I can't explain it, but I have this inkling.... Anyway, you should keep reading and translating. But, not right now."

"No?"

"No. You need a break."

"I'm fine. I just need—"

"You are not." He crossed his arms over his chest. "Don't think you can hide the dark circles under your eyes or how you yawn even after I know you've had at least two cups of tea when I arrive in the morning. You've been staying up late to work on the diary, haven't you?"

"I ..."

He tsked. "I meant what I said. I'll take the diary away if I have to. You must get some rest."

"But I'm not tired," she complained, as if she were a child being coaxed to take a nap.

"Then you must find something else to do."

"Like what?"

"Read a book—no wait," he chuckled. "Your eyes must be nearly falling out of their sockets from reading. You can take a walk or perhaps a swim? The beach is about a twenty-minute walk from here."

"I'm afraid I don't have anything to wear, unless you want me to swim naked."

Thoralf's face turned the most delightful shade of red. "Er, I s-suppose not," he stammered.

Oh dear, was he embarrassed? Of thinking of her naked? The very idea brought a thrill to her. Perhaps she was so emboldened that the next words just flew out of her mouth without thought. "I know something I can do—give you a haircut."

"Excuse me?" Now he turned practically purple.

"No offense, Thoralf, but you're badly in need of some grooming." She wrinkled her nose. "And when was the last time you had a shave?"

"I make do when I can," he declared, though his tone was defensive. "I don't often have time when I'm traveling."

"So let me do it for you. I've been trimming my own hair, as well as my father's, since I was thirteen. Surely yours isn't that much more difficult. I can clean up your beard too, if you want, or shave it down if you can get me a razor."

"Er, that's really not necessary," he said.

"I thought you said I should do something else aside from reading?"

"Don't you have any hobbies? Interests?"

"Out here? What am I supposed to do? Needlework?" She chuckled as she marched him to the bathroom. "Now, go and wash your hair and your face, then take a fresh towel and sit in the armchair in the living room." Pushing him inside the bathroom, she grinned before she shut the door. "Don't take too long now."

Heading toward her bedroom, Willa retrieved her scissors from the top drawer of her dresser. *Oh dear, what did I just do?*

Well, it was too late now, a voice inside her answered. *You practically bullied the man.*

Scrounging up all her courage, she headed out to the living room before she lost her nerve.

CHAPTER 7

As he settled down on the armchair, Thoralf already knew he was going to regret this.

Spending the last two days with Willa had been enjoyable to say the least. No, it was more than that. He couldn't quite remember the last time he'd looked forward to something. But when he woke up each morning, all he could think about was spending the day at the cottage, being near her and sitting down for their meal.

It was almost torture to have to leave her by afternoon. Part of him hoped she would invite him to stay for dinner, but he didn't want to impose. Besides, he promised Aleksei that he would come back before the end of each day to update him on the translations, as well as spend some time with him and Prince Harald. Though he was happy to be back with them, he thought of Willa every hour he wasn't near her, wondering what she was doing or if she was getting enough rest.

That logical part of his brain warned him not to get too close. That once she had her dragon back, she would likely go back to Fiorska or somewhere else. Maybe she would even want to start her own clan of Ice Dragons.

A stab of jealousy pierced through his gut like a knife. But he knew that was a possibility, especially from what she had told him about the Ice Dragons' attitude toward producing offspring. If she conceived a child with a human male, she would definitely give birth to an Ice Dragon.

If that was what she wanted, then she should have it. After all the pain and suffering she'd been through, Willa deserved all the happiness in the world.

His inner dragon scurried about, running in circles as if its tail had been set on fire.

What is the matter with you?

It snorted distastefully before settling down.

"Ready?" Willa asked as she entered the living area, a pair of golden scissors in her hand. "Don't worry, I won't cut you."

"I'm sure you have a steady hand." Leaning back, his gaze fixed on her as she approached him, his heart beating like a drum as she drew closer.

"Any preferences on style?"

"Whatever you think suits me best." It was difficult to think, having her so near that he could smell the sweet, floral scent of her soap and shampoo.

"All right." The smile she flashed him warmed his insides, and he released the death grip on the armchair. But when Willa reached out to run her fingers through his hair and scalp, he once again held on for dear life.

Mighty Odin, give me strength!

"Hmmm, let me see." She hummed as she continued to caress his hair, assessing it with her touch.

He forced his jaw to unclench as her nails massaged his scalp. It was soothing, really. No one had ever touched him in such an intimate way. There was nothing sexual about what they were doing, but there was a sensuality about it that sharpened his awareness. All he could focus on was the soft hums she made unconsciously, the touch of her fingers, and the heady smell of her. When she hovered over him to check the other side of his head, his eyes were treated to the swell of her breasts and her cleavage. His cock twitched involuntarily, and he bit the inside of his cheek.

Control yourself!

"Here we go," Willa announced.

Thoralf concentrated on the *snip, snip, snip* of the scissors, happy for the distraction. Still, as she continued to move closer and run her fingers over his scalp or lean against his shoulder for support, his control slipped little by little.

In their younger days, Aleksei would often tease him about his decision to wait to have sex with a woman. "You're too picky, my friend," he would say. "What are you waiting for?"

Thoralf didn't know how to answer that. Indeed, everyone around him was having sex. It wasn't that he didn't feel sexual desire or was completely innocent. He'd come close a few times, but ultimately the thought of a meaningless act lost appeal just before the act.

It wouldn't be meaningless with her.

"There you go," she declared.

"That was quick." He tried not to sound disappointed.

"The back and sides were just growing too long." Her fingers brushed his nape, picking out the small stray hairs stuck to his skin.

"Thank you, Willa." This torture was too much, so he made a motion to stand. However, her hand quickly moved to his shoulders.

"No, I'm not done with you yet." Her grip was surprisingly strong as she kept him in place. "Just let me trim the stray hairs on your beard for now."

Her touch mesmerized him, so he didn't protest when she pushed him back. However, instead of shifting to the side so she could get closer, she moved between his knees instead. Leaning forward, she stroked her thumb over his chin. "It's not too bad, really. Just a little overgrown."

When her fingers brushed over his lips, his cock hardened like steel.

Sweet Freya!

Her hips were only inches above him. He could pull her to his lap right this moment. As if it had a mind of its own, his hand reached out to her, brushing aside the hair falling over her arm to grab her and—

"*Stop.*" He drew his hand away. *What in Thor's name had he been thinking?*

Her mouth formed into a perfect O. "Is everything okay?"

Okay? She had no idea how close he had been to losing control. "I ... uh ..." Gently, he took her arm and guided her backward. "I must go."

Her expression faltered. "Go? Have I done something wrong? We don't have to trim—"

"No, no, you haven't done anything wrong." He swallowed hard. "Rorik ... is calling me. I must head to the palace for a meeting.

"Calling you?" Her nose wrinkled. "He can reach you all the way here from the palace?"

Damn. "He's flying overhead." Gods, he hated lying to her, but what he had wanted to do to her would have been worse. "Apologies, this meeting slipped my mind entirely. I must go, the king is waiting."

"I ... of course." She took a few steps back. "We can finish later."

"Er, sure." *Never.* The temptation was too much. If there was a next time, he didn't know if he'd be able to stop himself from mauling her.

"You'll come back tomorrow, right?" Ice blue eyes peered up at him. "At half past nine?"

How could he say no to her? His dragon practically shredded his insides at the thought of disappointing her. "I will."

"Good."

He murmured a goodbye and hastily made his exit, Cloaking himself before he took to the skies. His dragon let out a screech of protest, but he directed it upward and away from the cottage.

The fresh air did nothing to cool the desire in his blood. *I could have really embarrassed myself.* Or frightened Willa away and traumatized her. She didn't deserve that.

Yet, he could not promise himself to stay away from her. Besides, he was not done with his mission to reverse The Wand's effects and restore Prince Harald's dragon.

I cannot be alone with her. Not anymore. If they weren't alone, then it wouldn't be so bad. Perhaps she could continue her work at the palace. However, knowing Willa's aversion to leaving the cottage, she likely would not agree. That and she didn't like being around other people. Except ...

Your Majesty, he called to Queen Sybil as soon as he was within range of the mind link.

Thoralf? What is it?

I have a favor to ask, if you would indulge me.

A favor? Of course. What is it?

It's about Wi—Lady Willa.

Willa? Is she okay?

Yes. Thoralf paused as he carefully considered his words. *But I fear she's running herself into the ground. From what I can tell, she's been working day and night on the translations.* Not a lie, technically.

Oh dear, we can't have that, can we? the queen tsked. *What can I do to help?*

Perhaps tomorrow you can come with me, and you can convince her to take a break.

Oh, that actually sounds lovely. Queen Sybil chuckled. *And it's a good reason to leave the palace and Aleksei won't be able to forbid me.*

Thoralf smirked to himself. He knew Aleksei was extra protective of his mate, especially now that the queen was due to give birth to their second child any day. *I usually show up at the cottage around half past nine. Perhaps we could fly together?*

I might need a bit more time to get Alric ready, and Aleksei will never let me fly in my condition. Why don't you go ahead, and I'll have one of the staff take me. I'll try to arrive around that time.

He supposed that a few minutes alone with Willa

tomorrow wouldn't be so bad. *Of course. Are you sure I cannot assist you?*

No, no, I'll be fine. I've gone there lots of times with Alric.

I shall see you then, Your Majesty.

Thoralf breathed a sigh of relief. With the queen in the vicinity, surely he would be able to control himself around Willa.

Today had been too close. An innocent touch from Willa sent him near the edge. If he wasn't careful, he'd go tumbling right over it.

He was a bastard for thinking such thoughts about her. Willa had suffered enough. She didn't need unwanted attentions from a randy male. She was being nice, offering to help him with his hair and he nearly manhandles her.

Besides, my mission isn't complete, he told himself. *There was no time for anything else.* His honor was at stake.

The following day, Thoralf showed up a few minutes late at the cottage, hoping that Queen Sybil would be there ahead of him. To his surprise, the queen was nowhere to be found. Did she forget about their visit to Willa?

"You're here."

He couldn't ignore the sound of her voice as she exited the cottage, and he spun around to face her. Sparkling eyes like crystal and a bright smile greeted him. As always, her loveliness sent a warmth through him. This morning, however, she looked even more beautiful, with her hair flowing down her shoulders.

"Of course, did you think I would not show?"

The doubt on her face was fleeting, but he did not miss it. "You're late."

The light blue dress she wore enhanced the color of her eyes, but the shadows underneath them were unmistakable. "And you did not sleep again."

"I couldn't," she confessed. "Not until I knew she was okay after what happened."

Ephyselle. "And?"

The corner of her mouth perked up. "She had another child. A girl."

He had a feeling that was the case. When she started telling him about the priestess, a theory began to form in his mind, but he didn't want to share it with her yet, at least not until they had the full story. "That is wonderful news."

"I know." Her lips pursed together. "I wanted to ask you—"

The roaring of an engine cut her off. Frowning, Thoralf turned to the source of the sound. "What in Odin's name is going on?"

Two topless Jeeps came into view as they rounded the curve, heading toward them. He recognized them from the palace motor pool, so he didn't think they were in danger. But why were they here?

"Thoralf?" Willa asked. "Who are they?"

"It's ... the queen?" Her Majesty sat next to the driver in front of the first Jeep, while the other vehicle had—

"Are those children?" Willa squinted. "Looks like ... several of them."

"Yes, I believe so."

The Jeeps came to a halt a few feet from them, and the chorus of delighted screams filled the air.

"All right, children," Queen Sybil called. "Quiet down for a moment, please. Maya, dear, don't fuss with the seatbelt. Royce will help everyone out of their seats, but you must be patient."

Thoralf rushed to the queen's side when he saw her unbuckle her seatbelt. "Your Majesty. What a, uh, lovely surprise." *I'm afraid I didn't tell Willa you were coming*, he said to her privately.

She grinned at him. *Don't worry, I won't tell her you tattled.* "Willa, good morning."

Willa curtseyed and bowed her head in greeting. "Your Majesty. To what do I owe this visit?"

"Well, I woke this morning and thought, 'It's been so long since I've seen Willa,'" she said. "And Alric, too, hasn't seen you." She waved to the gurgling baby in the back seat. "You missed Willa, haven't you, darling?"

"Er, it's always good to see you, Your Majesty. And His Highness. And you brought guests."

"Yes, about that ..." She glanced around sheepishly. "See, Rorik and Poppy went on a mini honeymoon of sorts for the weekend. They're out camping in the outer islands, and they asked if I could watch Wesley." She nodded to the young dark-haired boy, about nine or ten years old, sitting next to the crown prince. "I said of course, and I thought, why not bring him to visit you? But then the other children heard about it, and they begged to come along. You don't mind, do you, Willa?"

Willa bit her lip. "I ... this is unexpected, and I have a lot of work to do—"

"Last one out's a rotten egg!" A young girl who was probably eight or nine years old raced out of the Jeep. "Haha!" She raised her fist in triumph. "I win!"

"No fair!" someone screamed. "You cheated by shifting!"

"Did not!"

"Maya," the queen called gently. "Can you come here for a moment?"

The girl skipped over to them, laughing maniacally. "Hello!"

Thoralf had met the audacious little ferret shifter the other day, along with the rest of Niklas's and Annika's brood. It was interesting, to say the least, and until now, he still could not believe that Niklas, of all people, had adopted five children.

"Lady Willa," Queen Sybil began. "This is Maya."

"Of House Aumont and Orven, Daughter of the Heart to Niklas of House Aumont and Annika Stormbreaker of House Orven," she added cheekily, then did a curtsey.

Willa chuckled. "Nice to meet you, Maya. Do forgive me for not using your whole title as it's the first time I've heard it. If you write it down, I promise to learn it."

"It's okay," she said. "It's a mouthful." Her tiny little face scrunched up as she assessed Willa. "Do you live out here by yourself? Why are you so far away? How come we've never seen you?"

"Oh, here's the rest of them," the queen announced quickly before Willa could react. "Let me introduce you. Come now, kids."

The children trudged forward and lined up in a neat row. Arne, the oldest, was actually Annika's adopted brother but was more like an older brother to the young ones. The twins, Eva and Elsie, came next, and they giggled as they curtseyed to Willa. Jakob, the youngest, was four and as they had apparently found out a few weeks ago, was a snake shifter. Finally, there was Wesley, Poppy's son. He was a quiet young man, a cheetah shifter according to Rorik.

"It's nice to meet you all," Willa said graciously. "Um, I guess I should go back and start working on the diary—"

"Nonsense." Queen Sybil nodded to the two drivers, who were now unloading several large wicker baskets from the back of the Jeeps. "Since it was such a lovely day, I thought we should have a picnic."

"A picnic?" Willa looked around nervously. "But I have so much work to do—"

The queen shook a finger her. "Nuh-uh. You're taking a break today," she declared.

"But the diary—"

"Will still be there tomorrow," the queen assured her. "Come on, let's eat. I'm starving."

Maya scurried up to Willa and grabbed her hand, threading their fingers together. "Do you like lemon cake, Lady Willa?"

"I do," she said. "It's my favorite."

"It's mine too!" She grinned at her. "I knew you were just like me and Mama. But why is your—"

"Me too!" Elsie added and took her other hand. "I like lemon cake like Mama and Lady Willa."

"And me!" echoed Eva, who grabbed onto her skirt.

Willa let out a throaty laugh as the three girls dragged her toward the picnic blankets spread out on the grass. The sound of her laughter warmed Thoralf's heart, as did the sight of her surrounded by children.

This is what she deserves. To have her dragon restored

and the clan reborn. It pained Thoralf to know that to do that, she would have to leave the Northern Isles.

His dragon, too, moaned woefully.

But he would not hold her back. He would do everything in his power to make it happen, no matter his personal feelings toward her. It was the right thing to do.

CHAPTER 8

After a sumptuous brunch prepared by the palace kitchen, the children were full of energy, so they played in the woods around the cottage. Thoralf offered to watch them so the queen and Willa could rest and chitchat. When they left, Willa assisted Queen Sybil in feeding Prince Alric and putting him down for a nap. Once the prince was snoozing, the two drivers brought over large pillows for them to relax on, and Willa went back to the cottage to make some tea.

"Is everything all right?" the queen asked as she reached out for the teacup she offered.

"All right?" Her hands shook, but thankfully Queen Sybil took the cup before it sloshed over any hot liquid. "Wh-what do you mean?"

"You just seem ... off. Did we disturb your peace? I'm really sorry, I had meant to come alone. Please forgive me for intruding on your privacy."

"No need for apologies, Your Majesty," she assured her. "I'm just ... overwhelmed."

Willa had done her best to hide the maelstrom of emotions she'd felt all morning, but it seemed the queen was more observant that she'd thought.

Thoralf's abrupt exit yesterday confused her. She was pretty sure he'd been lying about being called to the palace, but who was she to question him? But still, she knew something had changed between them yesterday.

Well, you did almost molest him.

She replayed the events for what seemed like a thousand times, and the memory of it never failed to make her cringe.

It wasn't like I could give him a haircut without touching him.

What had possessed her to be so bold? She had been practically on his lap. But, oh, she had loved massaging his scalp. At first, she thought he was enjoying himself too. But clearly, from the way he left, he'd been uncomfortable with her touch and the attention.

She shuddered in shame.

"Willa?" The queen waved her hand in front of her face.

"Er, yes?"

Queen Sybil pursed her lips, as if she were trying to say something, but changed her mind. "The children all together can be overwhelming. They are a handful, especially Niklas's kids."

"But they are all utterly charming and lively."

"They are. Maya especially—and speaking of which," she nodded ahead, to where the children and Thoralf were marching back toward them.

"The children have grown bored of the woods," Thoralf announced. "They want to play here instead."

"But what should we play?" Arne asked.

"Thoralf, do you know any traditional children's games?" the queen suggested. "Perhaps you can teach them one."

He thought for a moment. "Ah, indeed I do. It's one the king and I often played as children with the palace staff. Come, children!"

Willa's gaze never left him as he gathered the children close, knelt down, and began to explain the game by using a few pebbles he picked up from the ground. He seemed so patient with them, never condescending and never frustrated that they asked a lot of questions.

"He's so good with children," Queen Sybil remarked. "But I'm not surprised. Aleksei speaks highly of him, not just as a Dragon Guard."

She took a sip of tea to avoid having to comment.

"Lady Willa," Maya called her as she marched over to them. "We need another person on our team. Come join us!"

"What? Me?" Before Willa could protest further, the little girl grabbed her and pulled her to her feet. Her teammates—Eva and Wesley—cheered as she joined them. "I don't know the rules."

"They are very simple and easy to learn," Thoralf said.

The grin he sent her made her heart flip once again. "All right, tell me what to do."

He explained how the game worked to her: There were two teams who each had to protect a "base"—sticks buried in the ground. It was similar to capture the flag, but instead of taking an opponent's banner, one had to sneak past the defender to "touch" the base in order to win. There were also more rules about taking opponents captive by tagging them and saving your team members by tagging them back. There would be five rounds total, and everyone would have to rotate roles. The team who captured the base three times would win the game.

Soon, they started the game. Competition was quite fierce, even for a children's game, but she supposed that was natural especially with shifters.

"No fair!" Elsie cried when Maya changed into her ferret form to escape her grasp.

The furry little creature did a little jig and stuck its tongue out at her, and Elsie replied with an outraged shriek.

Thoralf raised his hand to halt the game. "All right, calm down, children." He bent down and shook his head at the ferret. "You're a slippery creature, aren't you?"

The animal replied with a series of chirps.

He chuckled. "I guess we didn't establish a no shifting rules, but we'll have to do it now so we can be fair to everyone. So, no more shifting or using shifter abilities."

They continued to play and after two rounds, the two teams were even. Willa was assigned to guard their base, so she stayed behind. Unfortunately, Thoralf was now one of the other team's invaders, so he came straight at their territory. With the final point on the line, she couldn't let her team down, even as he came barreling toward their base.

Blocking an opponent would have been enough because the defender could still capture an invader if they didn't touch the base first before they got tagged. However, with Thoralf's size and strength, she knew that wouldn't work, so she decided a more aggressive approach would be needed to scare him off. So, she spread her arms and charged right at him.

"Oh no you don't!" she shouted, grinning at him.

Thoralf's expression swiftly changed from fierce determination to surprise. "Willa, you must—"

She must have miscalculated his speed and distance as he did not have enough time to stop and turn. So instead, he careened right into her, sending her to the ground.

"Oomph!" Her back hit the grass with a soft thump. Before he landed on her, his arms encircled her waist, and they rolled around several times before she ended up on top of him. "Thoralf? Are you okay?"

He groaned. "Er, yes."

"Thank goodness." She relaxed, relieved he wasn't hurt. Big mistake as she melded against him, pressing into the firm, muscled planes of his body. "Oh ..." It felt so ... right, being here. Gazing into his midnight blue eyes, she saw a flash of emotion there.

"Willa ..."

A hand reached up to cup the side of her face.

"What are you guys doing?"

Maya's voice broke the spell, sending Willa scrambling off Thoralf. "I was, uh, defending our base."

Thoralf got to his feet. "Quite successfully too. I suppose I am now your captive."

Heat spread through Willa, curling through her lower stomach as wicked thoughts of Thoralf being her captive filled her imagination. Sparks practically flew as their eyes met, and once again, a furious blush colored the Dragon Guard's face.

"Why are you both red in the face?" Maya's eyes narrowed at them.

"It's all this running," Thoralf said quickly.

"Wh-why don't we declare a tie?" Willa suggested. "I'm

afraid I'm overheated from the exertion. I need some water." Cold water. Preferably an entire bucket to douse her overly stimulated body with.

They gathered the children, and they trudged back to the picnic blankets, where more snacks and refreshments were laid out.

"Your Majesty, I shall leave you to your—"

Queen Sybil clucked her tongue. "Oh no, Thoralf, please stay."

"But—"

The queen merely raised a dark eyebrow and pressed her lips together. Thoralf stood silently, so Willa guessed they must be having a private mind link conversation.

"I will stay," he relented, then sat at the farthest edge of the blanket, his shoulders tense and body stiff.

Willa wasn't sure which was better—to have him run away again after another close encounter with her or stay and deal with the awkwardness between them. Did she misread the interest in his eyes this time?

Yes, that had to be it. He clearly was not comfortable around her.

"I wanna sit beside Lady Willa," Eva said to Maya, who had taken up the space to her left.

"Nuh-uh." Maya scooted closer to Willa's side and wrapped an arm around her. "I was here first."

"But you already sat with her during lunch," Elsie protested. "Wes, will you switch with me?"

To her surprise, Wesley too, inched up to her right side, as if protecting his place next to her. "Uh, I guess you can sit over here," he said, indicating the seat on his right. Jakob, meanwhile, planted himself on Willa's lap and grinned up at her.

"Why do you guys get to sit with Lady Willa?" Eva complained.

"Duh, because we're all shifters," Maya said matter-of-factly. "And we stick together, right, Lady Willa?"

"Of cour—" She stopped short, feeling her stomach drop. That emptiness inside her taunted her, reminding her of what she had lost.

"H-how about lemon cake?" The queen stammered as she sent Willa an apologetic look.

"Yes, lemon cake!" Maya clapped her hands. "Our favorite."

When the young girl turned her innocent face up to her, Willa found the strength to speak, ignoring the heaviness pressing on her chest. "Yes." She managed a smile. "Our favorite. But we need some tea."

"Ooh, like a princess tea party!" Eva exclaimed.

"Exactly. Allow me to brew a fresh pot."

She didn't wait to be dismissed, and instead, gently pushed Jakob off her lap before hurrying back into the cottage. Once inside, she closed her eyes, trying to breathe in as much oxygen as she could.

It wasn't the child's fault. She probably couldn't tell that Willa's dragon was gone. Still, the reminder stung, even after she convinced herself that she had found peace.

Taking in another deep breath, she marched into the kitchen. Hopefully she would have composed herself by the time the water boiled.

"Willa."

Thoralf's soft bass calmed her nerves. "I'm just getting tea."

"She is a child, Willa. She didn't know."

"I know that." Spinning on her heel, she faced him. "Her words were said in innocence, not malice."

"I didn't realize someone had told them you were a shifter," he said. "Or that they knew anything about you before this."

Yes, that was strange indeed. "Perhaps the queen prepared the children for their visit here, but didn't know what to say." She shrugged. "It doesn't matter. I'll be fine."

"Of course it matters." He closed the distance between them. "I am sorry the children bothered you. I'll make sure no one comes here again without your express permission."

"Oh no, don't think I dislike the kids," she said. "That's not it. They're wonderful."

"But they bring you sadness. I can sense it."

She searched herself, wondering if his words were true. "No, not at all. Just a reminder."

"Of what?"

"Of the time before ... before what happened. I was reminded today of what I have lost." Her lower lip trembled, so she bit down on it.

"Willa, I'm so sorry." He took a step forward, nearly trapping her against the counter with his huge body. "You have lost a lot."

"I lost everything." The sob came despite her best efforts to stop it. "I have nothing."

"No, you have." His thumb brushed the tears from her cheek. "Grieve for what you've lost, but do not forget what you still have."

Slowly, she lifted her gaze to meet his midnight blue eyes. "And what is that?"

Willa braced herself as his head lowered toward her. Still, even if she had a hundred years, there was no way to prepare for what was about to happen.

His lips brushed over hers gently. The kiss was so soft, yet it was as if the world beneath her shifted. She drew her hands up and clutched at his shoulders to steady herself. Strong arms came around her waist, and she molded her body to his. Wanting to deepen the kiss, she parted her mouth and licked at his lips. Spicy and sweet at the same time, but just a taste wasn't going to satisfy her. She wanted more. All that he could give.

"Willa, I'm so—oh my God!"

They broke apart at the sound of Queen Sybil's voice. Thoralf staggered back as Willa braced herself on the kitchen counter, panting heavily.

The queen's eyes were as wide as saucers as she stood in the doorway. "I, um. Wanted to check on you. But I see you're, er, busy. I'll be outside."

Once she heard the sound of the cottage door slam shut, she turned to Thoralf. "So ..."

"We should talk," he said.

"Y-yes." Was he going to tell her their kiss was a mistake? It certainly didn't feel like one. In fact, to her, it was the exact opposite of a mistake. He was the one who leaned down, but maybe he'd meant to give her a friendly hug? Even now, she could sense his hesitation. She straightened her shoulders. "I'm sorry."

"Sorry?"

"For taking advantage of you and your kindness." Yes,

that was it, right? He was a nice person, that was evident from how he'd done all the repairs for the cottage. After all, it couldn't have been just because she was doing the translations. "My advances weren't intentional, but I would be lying if I said I didn't feel attraction to you. You've just been too polite to tell me off, but clearly, I've made you uncomfortable with how I touch you, and now, this kiss. I apologize, and it won't happen again."

"It's hardly taking advantage of me if I wanted you too."

"We can—what?" Her head snapped up to meet his gaze.

"I thought I was the one taking advantage of you." Midnight blue eyes sparkled with amusement before they softened into warmth. "Yesterday, when you were touching me, I could barely control myself. The things I thought of and wanted to do ... they were not appropriate."

Heat curled in her belly, wondering how inappropriate his thoughts were. "You never indicated you were interested in me."

"You are a guest of my king," he continued. "And it would not be honorable of me to take advantage of you, especially since you are doing us a great service."

"I'd be benefitting from helping with the diary, too, you know," she pointed out.

"True, but it wasn't a task you initially wanted. And as I spent more time with you, I couldn't help myself. I felt drawn to you." Color heightened in his cheeks. "My king tasked me to aid and watch over you. It would be ungentlemanly of me to make advances, not to mention, you are still grieving over your loss."

She could see how he would think it was improper for him to act on his attraction. "I wasn't sure how I felt about you. At first, I was annoyed. I was content with my life here, and then you come along ... I didn't want to hope. Three years, and I barely let anyone in. But somehow, you got past my defenses." She smiled up shyly at him. "I thought you were just hanging around here to do work on the cottage."

"True, but I also wanted to be near you." As if to prove his point, he took a step closer to her. "I do want you. But also. to be with you." He swallowed audibly. "But I also want to restore your dragon."

"Why would being with me and getting my dragon back be mutually exclusive?"

"Because once did, you would leave the Northern Isles. Reclaim your land." His jaw tensed. "Rebuild your clan by having children with another man. I would not be able to bear it. To let you go to be with another. But I would never stop you from seeking your happiness and doing your duty."

All the air in Willa's lungs rushed out. He didn't want her to be with someone else?

"You are the last of your kind," he continued. "Of course you must do everything in your power to restore your clan."

He wasn't wrong. If at anytime these past three years she had her dragon back, that's exactly what she would have done. She owed it to her father and the others who died.

But now, she wasn't so sure.

The loud rapping on the door startled them both. "Thoralf? Are you in there?"

He muttered a curse under his breath.

"Can we come in?"

"It's Gideon," he explained to her. "It might be urgent."

"Then you should talk to him." It was rotten timing.

There was so much left unsaid, but it would give her time to gather her thoughts and think about Thoralf's words.

"Come in," she called out.

Gideon entered the kitchen moments later, followed by a young blonde woman. Willa recognized her from the other day when they all came to her. "Hello," she greeted.

"Willa, you know Gideon. This is Ginny Russel, his mate," Thoralf introduced.

Ginny nodded at her. "Hello, Lady Willa." Her accent was similar to the queen's, which meant she, too, was American.

"What is it?" Thoralf said to Gideon.

"I have some news. It's about the Knights." His golden amber eyes briefly darted to Willa. "We should talk in private."

"You can speak freely in front of me," Willa said.

Gideon looked to Thoralf, who nodded in agreement. "All right. Actually, I did want to speak to Lady Willa on another matter, so that would save me time."

Why would the Dragon Guard seek her out? "You need to speak to me?"

"Yes. But first let's take care of other business. Ginny?"

"I'll get straight to the point," Ginny began. "The Agency has discovered the location of the Knights' lab where they make Formula X-87."

Thoralf's nostrils flared. "That vile substance ... we must destroy it then."

"Agreed. The location is just off the coast of Malta so the main headquarters in Lykos is taking point on this one. Christina asked that we work with her brother, Xander

Stavros. He's requested air support, and King Aleksei said he'd send two Dragon Guards."

"Of course. I will go," Thoralf said.

"Stein will accompany you," Gideon added.

"Wait," Willa reached out to Thoralf, grabbing his hand. "You're leaving?"

"I must. Destroying this lab would be a major blow to the Knights and save many shifter lives."

She bit her lip. "It sounds dangerous."

"It is my duty." He squeezed her hand. "I have tangled with the Knights before and overcome them."

What was she supposed to do or say? It wasn't like she could tell him not to go. "Be safe, then."

"I will."

"We need to go soon," Ginny interrupted. "Within the hour."

Her heart sank. She didn't think he would be leaving so soon.

"Then I must prepare," he said. "But first, why did you need to speak with Willa, Gideon?"

"Ah, right. Lady Willa," he began. "Thoralf mentioned that you'd been translating the book manually, correct?"

"With pen and paper, yes."

"Well, I think there may be a way to speed things along."

"How?"

"Using machine translation. I've done something similar with some old diaries written in our old language," he explained. "When you initially declined to translate the book, I had thought of doing the same, but we didn't have any reference material to compare. However, now that you've done a chunk of the translation, we could actually input your work and scan the contents of the diary and the computer will do the translating of the runes you've already worked on."

"I didn't think that was possible." While she loved reading Ephyselle's words, it was a tedious task. Sometimes it would take her over an hour to translate just one sentence.

"It's not perfect and you would still need to go over the machine translations and make corrections. But the program works in a way that it learns from its mistakes and the process gets faster as we go along. We can even just do a search for relevant keywords and find references to Aristaeum and the temple. But that would mean you'd have to come to the palace and work with me in the library."

"Oh." Which would mean leaving the cottage and being around other people.

"You don't have to do anything you don't want to," Thoralf assured her. "You can keep doing things as you were."

She thought for a moment. It seemed almost sacrilegious to just hand over Ephyselle's personal writings to a machine. *But on the other hand, we would find the answers we need right away.* "I'll do it."

"Great," Gideon said.

Thoralf squeezed her hand. "If you think that's the way to go, I support it."

"We really need to go soon," Ginny reminded them.

"I need a moment," Thoralf said. "If you please."

"Of course."

Once Ginny and Gideon left, Thoralf turned to face her. "I will be back."

"I know you will." Her chest tightened involuntarily. She didn't want to be apart from him, but he had his orders. "Take care and good luck."

"Thank you. And I will see you soon."

Disappointment filled her when he stepped back and gave her respectful nod of the head before turning to leave. She'd hoped for more, even a friendly hug.

Maybe it was better they didn't act on their attraction. She couldn't promise him that she wouldn't leave if she did get her dragon back. She was Alpha of the Ice Dragons, and her clan was her first priority.

"Lady Willa! Lady Willa!"

The sound of footsteps jolted her out of her thoughts. "Oh, hello, Maya."

The little girls sauntered up to her. "We were all waiting for you to come back and then the queen went to get you. But she came back and said you and Thoralf needed some time to talk." Her small eyebrows drew together. "We weren't supposed to disturb you, but I saw Thoralf leave with Uncle Gideon and Aunt Ginny, so I thought that meant you were done talking, so I came to get you."

"Oh, uh, yes. Did you need something?"

Maya grinned at her then pulled something out of her pocket. "I saved you a piece of lemon cake."

Willa laughed. "You're very kind, thank you." As she took the half-crumbled cake from the child's hands, she decided that for now, she would put any negative thoughts aside. Thoralf would be back soon, plus, she had to continue working on the diary. "Why don't we go outside and join everyone else? It's such a wonderful day, and it's not over yet."

Taking Maya by the hand, they went outside and joined the others. The queen and the children stayed for a few more hours, and when it was time to go, they were more than reluctant to leave.

"Will you come visit us at the palace, Lady Willa?" Eva asked.

"Actually, I'll be working at the library tomorrow," she replied. "Perhaps you can come for some tea and lemon cake?"

"I'll have a car sent up to get you in the morning," Queen Sybil said.

The queen didn't say a word about the kiss she had witnessed in the kitchen, which Willa appreciated. "Thank you."

She saw them off, waving goodbye as they drove off. Once they were gone, she turned back toward the cottage. Without the sounds of the children, the entire place was so silent—unnervingly so. And without the distraction of their presence, she had a long night ahead of her. For the first time in a long time, Willa reached out to the skies in prayer.

Goddess, keep him safe.

CHAPTER 9

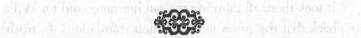

A car showed up at her doorstep the next day to bring her to the palace. She had already packed up Ephyselle's diary, her notes, as well as the laptop, so she was ready to go. Soon, they arrived at the palace, and Gideon met her at the entrance and they headed toward the library.

"Sorry, it's bit of a mess in here," Gideon said as they entered one of the small rooms in the back. "This was a reading room that we converted into our office." The space was smaller than her living area in the cottage with two desks squished together in the back that had several monitors and wires running into CPUs underneath. One wall had a whiteboard that was covered in charts, maps, and photos. There was another table on the opposite side that had a scanner and a laptop, which Gideon pointed out. "We'll be working here."

Gideon explained, perhaps in the simplest of terms, of how the program worked. First, they would scan the diaries and her notes, and the program he created would match the runes to their translations. After that, she would look over the computer's work and make any corrections. Once they finished her notes, the program could then start the automated translations, which Willa would also have to check and correct. In theory, as the program compiled more information, the translations would be quicker and more precise.

"This is genius work," she remarked. "And I have to say, I won't miss having to do this all by hand."

"Let's get started."

It took them all morning to scan her notes and for Willa to check that the runes matched their translations. In truth, she was glad for the distraction. She hardly slept a wink last night, thinking about Thoralf and where he was and what he could be doing. But she could only hope and pray their mission was successful.

She finished working on the last page when the familiar scent of fresh brewed tea tickled her nostrils.

"You looked like you could use a cup." Gideon raised the two mugs in his hand and then offered her one.

"Thank you," she replied with a yawn. Grateful, she took the cup and had a sip. "I did need one."

"Couldn't sleep last night?"

She nodded.

"Neither could I," he confessed. "It's the first time Ginny's been away on a mission without me."

"Oh." She recalled Thoralf had introduced the woman as Gideon's mate. "You must be worried about her."

"Yeah, but I know she's all right."

"You've heard news?" In her excitement, she sloshed tea over the side of the mug. "Oh Goddess, I'm sorry."

"No worries." Gideon reached for a paper towel and quickly mopped up the spill. "And no, I haven't heard from them. They'll be on blackout until they return."

Willa wrapped her hands around the mug. "Then how could you be so sure she's all right?"

A wistful smile spread across his face. "Right here." He tapped his chest. "Through our bond. I know she's alive and well."

"Your bond?"

"You haven't heard about the bond between fated mates?"

Willa wrinkled her nose. "I've heard about the concept of fated mates, but as far as I knew, no one in my clan had ever met theirs." She gestured to the book. "Except Ephyselle, apparently." She gave him a brief background of what she'd read so far. "We live so far away and our population is so small, so maybe the chances of us meeting our mates would have been very low."

"I understand." His brows furrowed. "I never would have met Ginny if she didn't come here in the first place."

Unable to help herself, she asked, "Did you know right away she was your mate?"

"Oh yeah," he chuckled. "My dragon told me she was mine, and her lioness did the same. She actually met Niklas first, and then she ran into me thinking I was him and her animal told her."

"I didn't realize Ginny was a shifter too. A lioness? Do you not mind?"

"Mind what?"

"That—oh, I'm sorry." She bit her lip. "It's rather forward of me to ask such a personal question."

"No, I don't mind." Golden eyes pinned her. "Go ahead."

"Well ... any children you produce will be lions or lionesses, right?"

"True. And?"

"You don't want dragon children?"

"I want children with Ginny," he stated firmly. "I don't care what they are, as long as they're ours." The conviction in his voice was evident.

"Of course. I don't mean to offend."

"I'm not offended, Lady Willa," he assured her. "It's difficult to explain how the mate bond works and how it enhances our relationship. To me, Ginny is the reason I live and breathe. She could give me a dozen cubs or none at all, and I would still think the sun rises and sets with her. I feel her, here, in my heart."

The words made Willa's throat tighten. "That's wonderful." How amazing it must be to have such a connection to someone.

"We don't need to be mates to be with someone, you know. Lots of people fall in love without it. I know that even if we weren't mates when we met, I would have fallen for Ginny just the same. I love her because she's her, not because we're mates."

The way his golden eyes pierced right into her when he said those words unnerved her. Unable to bear his gaze, she quickly turned around. "We should get back to—"

"He cares for you."

She blinked involuntarily.

"And you care for Thoralf."

There was no use lying. "I do."

"Then what's holding you back?"

She whirled around to face him. "It's complicated." Now that was an understatement.

"In all the years I've known him, Thoralf's never had a

relationship or has been serious about anyone," Gideon said. "But you're different. If you both care for each other, then you should be together."

"It's not me who's holding back," she said icily.

Surprise flashed across his face. "I ... see. Forgive me for overstepping my bounds."

"It's fine." Biting her lip, she turned away from him again. It really shouldn't be complicated, right? Attraction, sex, procreation. The Ice Dragon way was much simpler. They were attracted to each other, and as consenting adults, she and Thoralf should be able to jump into bed if they wanted. If they were both Ice Dragons living in Fiorska, no one would bat an eye; they'd even be encouraged.

But she'd replayed his words over and over again and came to a conclusion: He didn't want to get hurt.

I would not be able to bear it. To let you go to be with another.

And he had every right to protect himself.

A human male would be a guarantee that she'd produce an Ice Dragon heir. Of course, that was the right choice.

Or perhaps those were all excuses. Maybe Thoralf didn't want to be with her. Maybe, like his friends, he was waiting for his fated mate.

The very thought plunged her into despair, and she had a nonsensical urge to claw out the eyes of this unknown woman out there who Thoralf belonged to.

"Lady Willa—" A ringing sound interrupted Gideon, and the mood in the room shifted. "That's Ginny."

Finally, some news. She followed Gideon as he pushed his office chair back toward the computer behind him. He clicked on the mouse and the lioness shifter's face filled the screen as it lit up.

"Thank Thor," Gideon exhaled. "You're all right."

"I am, and so is Stein."

The tension on her face, however, was evident, and Willa immediately knew something was wrong. "Where's Thoralf?"

"He's—Lady Willa? You're there?"

"We're working on the translation," Gideon explained. "But what about Thoralf?"

Her lips pressed together. "You should get His Majesty on this call. He needs to hear—"

"Tell me now," Willa interrupted. "Please."

Ginny hesitated for a moment. "He's alive, but badly injured. The mission was a success, and they didn't know we were coming, but they were obviously prepared for any attack. The island was equipped with anti-aircraft missiles, and one of them hit Thoralf's dragon. Thankfully, by that time we'd already secured the lab. and Stein was able to fish him out of the water. He's being transported to Lykos as we speak."

"I need to see him," Willa said.

Ginny shook her head. "I'm afraid that's not possible. You need special permission to enter Lykos. Besides, according to the medic, he should fully recover in a day or so. He'll be home soon enough if you just be patient."

"No." She didn't know why, but she had to see he was alive with her own eyes. "I must see him as soon as possible. Please, Ginny."

She hesitated for a moment. "I'll talk to my boss. But I'm

not promising anything. Xander Stavros doesn't like ... outsiders."

"Of course, do what you can." Not that Willa cared what this Stavros person thought. One way or another, she would find a way to see Thoralf.

"I'll get back to you as soon as I can," Ginny said before the screen went blank.

"He'll be fine," Gideon assured her. "Thoralf's tough. If he didn't die instantly, that means all he needs is a few hours rest before his body heals."

"I know." Her mind told her that too. But her gut screamed that she had to see him now. Her chest tightened. She hated how they had parted yesterday. So many things unsaid, the doubt widening the gap between them. Was he even asking her to choose him or stating what he thought she would do?

None of that mattered now, only that she see, touch, and feel him, to tell herself that he was fine and alive.

"Do you want to go back to the cottage? You can get some rest. I'll send word if I hear anything else."

"No." She didn't want to risk missing any further news. "I could use the distraction."

"All right."

They went back to work, though that really meant sitting and waiting for Willa. She watched the screen, waiting for the program to tell her if it read a rune it didn't know the translation for, and she provided the answer. Still, it helped pass the time and eventually, the program had completed a whole paragraph without her assistance.

Fiorska, Twenty-seventh Round of the Moon, Five Hundred and Fith Cycle of Makinen

I have received word that my tribe's old enemy, the vile Wizard Aristaeum, is up to his old tricks.

"Gideon!" Excitement pounded in her chest.

"What is it?" The Dragon Guard was behind her in an instant. "Did you find something?"

"Yes." She waved the printed page in his face. "A reference to Aristaeum, finally. She called him her tribe's old enemy." Something clicked in her mind. "He must have been the one that attacked her tribe in the first place, when Gustav came to rescue her. She never names him until now." She pointed to the runes that translated to his name.

"That's fantastic." Pulling the laptop to face him, he leaned down and tapped on the keys. "I'm going to add a line of code that highlights whenever the runes that refer to him pop up. That should speed things along."

It seemed so close now. But, she couldn't even celebrate because she was still worried about Thoralf. How was he doing now? Where was he? Was he comfortable? Did someone watch over him while he healed?

"Gideon? Lady Willa?"

"Your Majesty." Gideon got to his feet and placed his hand over his chest before bowing.

"King Aleksei," Willa greeted, but when she made the motion to stand, the king waved at her.

"I'll be brief." His expression was grave, the lines on his face deepening as if in thought. "Ginny explained to me what happened and your request to see Thoralf, Lady Willa."

"And?"

"Xander Stavros is a stubborn *sonofabitch*—pardon my language—but my wife intervened on your behalf using their family connection." He quickly explained that Queen Sybil's brother was married to Stavros's sister. "He has given you permission to come to Lykos. His plane will be here to pick you up in four hours."

"Pick me up?"

"The location of Lykos is secret, so he won't allow anyone else to bring you there. And you must go alone."

The idea of boarding a stranger's plane to go to a secret location should have unnerved her, but the prospect of possibly seeing Thoralf made her fears dissipate. "Thank you, Your Majesty."

The king's ocean-colored eyes narrowed, as if assessing her. Willa could tell he wanted to make a comment about ... whatever it was between herself and Thoralf, but he merely said, "Please take care of Thoralf. He is like the brother I never I had."

"I will, Your Majesty. Also, I'd like to thank the queen personally before I go."

"She is resting now, but if you do not see each other, I will relay your gratitude." He looked at Gideon, and they exchanged knowing glances before he left the library.

"I'm glad you'll be able to see him, my lady," the Dragon Guard said.

"Me too. But—oh! I can't let you do all the work while I'm away. I mean, I probably won't be long." If Thoralf was okay—no, she knew he was going to be fine—maybe she would just stay a few hours, and once he recovered, they could come to the Northern Isles right away.

"Don't worry about it. The machine can do most of the work while you're gone, and when you get back you can look it over."

She smiled warmly at him. "I don't know how to thank you, Gideon."

"There is a way."

"How?"

"Talk to Thoralf and tell him how you really feel."

She flinched. Did she even know she felt about him now? Would he have changed his mind?

I almost lost him.

If that missile had hit his heart or brain, he would have died instantly, and then he wouldn't have known how strong her feelings were. That she was going to choose *him*. "I promise, I will."

The private jet arrived at the airstrip just outside the capital city of Odelia on time. To Willa's relief, Ginny was already waiting inside when she got in there.

"How is he?" were her first words to the lioness.

"Not great when I saw him." Ginny nodded to the seat next to her. "Stein dragged him to shore. The wound was too big, and he had to remain in dragon form until he came back to consciousness. That's when Stavros offered to bring him to Lykos so his healers could work on him."

Her lips pursed. "Who is this Xander Stavros?"

"Alexander Stavros is the Beta and son of Ari Stavros, Alpha of the Lykos Wolves," Ginny began. "That's The Agency's big boss. Rumor has it Ari wants to retire soon, which means Xander's gonna take over as Alpha. Some might think him cold and cruel, but that's how you have to be when you're going to take over one of the world's largest wolf packs."

Willa understood that, having been trained for leadership herself. And normally, she wouldn't even be intimidated by any shifter if she had her dragon, but it sounded like the wolf was a force to be reckoned with. Besides, this Xander Stavros couldn't be that bad if he offered to help with Thoralf's recovery.

The rest of the three-hour flight was silent. Willa was too wired to rest or even relax. All she could think about was Thoralf. When the plane began to descend, the razor wire seemingly wrapped around her throat loosened.

"I guess we're here," Ginny said when the plane touched down and the engine powered down. There was no staff on board to tell them what was going on, no announcements or welcome greetings from the pilot. The message from Stavros was evident: they were not guests.

The door to the plane opened and two figures came in wearing matching dark suits, though one was a hulking blond man and the other was a tall, equally menacing-looking woman.

"Stand," the woman commanded. They did as they were told. "Surrender any weapons you have now."

"I don't have any—hey!" Ginny growled when the woman grabbed at her waist. "Watch it!"

"If you do not subject yourselves to a search, this plane will return you to where you came from."

Ginny grumbled but allowed the woman to search her. She did the same to Willa, and once the inspection was done, she told them in a gruff voice to follow her. They descended the stairs of the plane and were ushered into an SUV. The tinting on the windows was so dark Willa couldn't even tell that it was daytime outside.

They drove for about half an hour before the vehicle slowed, taking winding roads down what Willa could tell were steep cliffs overlooking the ocean. When the door opened and she stepped out, she let out an audible gasp.

"It's …" she trailed off, unable to find words to describe the sight before her.

To their right was a beautiful white villa surrounded by pink and white shrubbery, but that wasn't what had her nearly speechless. They were standing right by the powdery white shore leading into the sparkling blue ocean. The warm sun felt so good on her skin, and Willa closed her eyes, breathing in the salty air. Such places existed only in her imagination, and now she was here.

"Lioness, you said she was a shifter," came the rough, cutting voice like the edge of a knife.

Willa spun around. A tall, imposing man appeared in the doorway of the villa. Even from a distance, she could feel his dominant, dark stare. This had to be Xander Stavros.

"Humans are not permitted on Lykos." Those dark eyes bore into her. "And I will not let a human near any shifter in a vulnerable state."

Ginny opened her mouth to speak, but Willa raised a hand to stop her. While she appreciated that Stavros wanted to protect Thoralf, he was also attempting to keep her from him. That she couldn't accept.

"I am no human," she announced.

His cruel mouth twisted. "But you have no animal."

"Because of The Wand," she stated.

If he felt any sympathy toward her, he didn't show it.

"But make no mistake. Once I have my dragon back, I will take my rightful place as Alpha of the Ice Dragons." She said it with so much conviction, she even believed it herself.

The wolf snorted, clearly not intimidated. "The foolish water dragon saved my life and that of my wolves, and thus I owe him a debt. As he drifted in and out of consciousness, he called one name. Over and over again." His mouth spread into an approximation of a smile, showing off perfect white teeth against tanned olive skin. "You must be Willa."

Her heart leapt into her throat. "I am."

He crossed his arms over his wide chest, but stepped aside. "He is asleep in the bedroom. The doctors said he needs his–hey!"

She didn't need further invitation. Ignoring the foreign curses Stavros called after her, she dashed into the villa. She wasn't sure how, but she located the master bedroom easily. Stopping short by the doorway, her breath caught in her throat.

Thoralf lay in the middle of the large bed, a white sheet pulled up to his waist. White bandages covered one side of his torso and his skin was paler than snow.

"Thoralf ..." She walked to his side and sat on the bed.

Reaching over, she took his hand in hers. His eyes were closed, but his breathing was steady.

He was going to be all right. She breathed a sigh of relief and nearly wept. But she had to see it for herself. Crawling over, she tucked herself into his side, curling her body into a ball, then allowed exhaustion to pull her into sleep.

CHAPTER 10

Thoralf felt like he'd been hit by a freight train.

Actually, he'd been hit by a freight train once, and this worse than that. His head pounded like someone was hitting it with a hammer. He tried to move, but the pain in his side made it impossible to do so. Not that he had the strength to move. He couldn't even open his eyes.

However, through the pounding and the pain, he could scent something familiar. The faint, flowery smell of shampoo and soap.

Willa.

Maybe he was dead. Or dying. Of course she'd be the person he'd be thinking of before he left this earth. His thoughts were filled with her all the time, after all.

Willa. Beautiful, strong, kind and lovely Willa.

Do not grieve me, my Willa.

Then everything went dark again.

Thoralf wasn't sure when he woke next, but he felt remarkably better. His eyes fluttered open, and for brief moment, sunlight blinded him. "*Ugh.*" He raised a hand to block out the light.

"You're awake!"

Willa?

The bed shifted, and he dropped his hand. Blinking the blurriness away, he looked up and stared into a pair of familiar ice blue eyes. "You're here—*oomph*!"

"Thoralf," she cried as she embraced him and plastered her face into the crook of his neck. "I'm so glad you're awake."

She really was here. And he wasn't dead. His brain scrambled to put together what happened. *The operation to destroy the lab.*

They had been successful in destroying the Knight's secret island facility, but they had failed in securing the island properly. There was a secret bunker on the other side, and as they prepared to leave, Thoralf saw the land-to-air missile headed straight for the helicopter that carried Xander Stavros and his team. With no choice left, he quickly shifted and blocked the missile.

"Thoralf? Are you okay?"

He jolted back to the present. *Willa.* His arms came around her and pulled her close. "I thought you were a dream." He inhaled that sweet scent of her. Snippets from the past few hours flickered into his mind. Stein carrying him back to shore. Being lifted into the helicopter. The healers telling him he was safe in Lykos and that he needed sleep in order to heal. He tightened his hold. "I can't believe you're here."

"Yes, I'm here." She shifted onto her side, snaking an arm over his chest and laying her head on his shoulder.

He frowned. He couldn't believe Xander Stavros allowed

her to come to Lykos; the wolf pack was notoriously xenophobic and never allowed visitors on their territory.

On his quest, he'd encountered the Greek wolf several times, working with him on some occasions. Though the future Alpha was gruff and direct, Thoralf respected him; he was a fair leader and ruthlessly efficient. He also despised weakness. He wondered what Willa did that he let her come here, because he knew no amount of begging and pleading would have made the indomitable Alpha bend the rules.

"I thought ... I thought you'd ..."

Sensing her distress, he rolled to his side, then tipped her face up to meet his gaze. "I'm fine. All healed. Were you worried about me?"

"Of course I was, silly." Her voice hitched even as she tried to sound casual. "I didn't like the way things ended between us."

"I didn't either." He cupped her face, rubbing his thumb over her cheek. "I meant everything I said. I will restore your dragon, Willa."

"I know." She closed her eyes. "But it wasn't about that." Long lashes fluttered before her icy blue gaze pinned him. "I understand what you were trying to say to me, you know. But I never got a chance to reply."

He smiled weakly. "You have a duty to your clan."

"But it's not just that, is it?" Her lips tightened. "You're afraid of getting hurt."

"Hurt?"

"You said it yourself. You couldn't bear the thought of me being with someone else. You thought I would reject you, just like my clan did."

All the air left his lungs, leaving only a familiar pain.

"You didn't even give me a chance," she continued. "And did you even consider that you could hurt me too?"

"I would never hurt you," he stated firmly.

She smiled weakly. "What about your fated mate? Once you meet her, you'll leave me."

His very being denied it, but he had to face facts. When a shifter met their mate, the need to bond would always be there, their animal driving the need to claim and bond. "I wouldn't be cruel to you."

"But you'd hurt me just the same."

"Willa," he began gently. "I don't even know if I would ever meet my mate or if she even exists. Only a small percentage of shifters meet their fated mates, and many of our kind form happy unions with people who are not their mates. Take my parents for example. I would never just walk away from you if my mate came along."

"Yet you seem to think I would do the same once I get my dragon back."

"I—" He snapped his mouth shut. She'd got him there. "You're right."

"Of course I am," she said matter-of-factly. "Thoralf, I hate this idea that someday, someone could come along and take you away from me. But at the same time, I can't deny my feelings for you any longer. And you know what? I'm willing to take that chance. Because I want to know what it's like to be with you."

"What about your duty to your clan?"

"I don't even know if I'll get my dragon back. Just like you don't know if you'll find your mate. So, are we just supposed to stay away from each other because we're afraid of getting hurt?" The corner of her lip tugged up. "Someone once told me that we aren't supposed to skip the sad parts."

Thoralf stared at her, completely awed.

"Besides, I would love and cherish any child you gave me, Ice Dragon or not."

Emotion swelled in him, as well as something primal at the thought that she could someday carry his child. Overwhelmed, he captured her mouth with his.

She moaned and pressed her soft curves into his body. The need to taste her, possess her exploded within him, and he rolled over on top of her. He deepened the kiss, tugging at the side of her mouth to part her lips so he could slip his tongue inside and taste her.

Her hips shifted, and he only realized that he was naked underneath the sheet when his cock went hard and brushed against her hip. Reluctantly, he pulled away.

"Thoralf?" she panted. "What's wrong? Don't you want—"

"I want you," he interrupted. "Never doubt that. But there's something you should know."

Concern marred her face. "What is it?"

"I have ... never been with anyone before."

"Never been—oh." Her eyes widened. "Never?"

"Ever."

"You're a virgin?"

He nodded. "Not that I never had the chance or interest. I've just been too focused on my duties and trying to be the best Dragon Guard I could be. There was no time for relationships."

"Oh."

"Do you mind?" Anxiety flooded his chest. "Are you disappointed?"

"What? No, no." She reached up and cupped the sides of his face. "Not at all. I'm just surprised." She bit her lip. "Do you mind that I'm not a virgin?"

"Well, one of us has to know what they're doing." He chuckled, then kissed the furrow between her eyebrows. "You are perfect as you are." Taking her mouth again, he kissed her deeply, their tongues tangling in a desperate attempt to taste and devour each other. When they pulled away, he said, "I want to touch you."

"You can touch me anywhere." Her fingers reached between them to unbutton the front of her dress, exposing an expanse of creamy white skin and full breasts tipped with hard pink nipples. "Thoralf ..."

Unable to help himself, he cupped one breast, feeling its weight in his hands and teasing the tip with his thumb. She gasped and arched her back, offering herself to him. So, he leaned down and took the other tip into his mouth, sucking it in deep and making her moan aloud.

"More ... please, Thoralf, touch me more."

He flipped her around again so they lay on their sides, her back pressed up to his chest. He moved his hand down and slipped them inside her panties, then stroked the fine curls between her thighs. To his surprise, she was already wet. She bit her lip when his fingers rubbed up and down her lips, parting them and pressing his fingers into her.

"Thoralf ..." Her hips undulated against his hand, and he slipped a finger deep into her. She was so warm and inviting, and his cock rubbed against the soft flesh of her buttocks painfully. When he pulled his finger out, she moaned in disappointment, which turned into a groan of pleasure when his thumb found her clit.

"How do you like it? Like this?" He stroked the nub in a slow and steady manner that had her mewling. "Or like this?" He positioned her clit between two fingers and rubbed harder.

"Like that!" Her hips bucked up toward him. "Please ... I need ..."

He didn't want to make her wait, so he continued with the fast, rough strokes until her body shuddered with a quick orgasm. "Beautiful."

She twisted her body around to face him. "I need you, Thoralf. Inside me. Please."

Her words sent his cock twitching, so he pulled the sheet away as she slipped her panties off.

"Can I touch you?"

He nodded, then held his breath. Her touch was light as she wrapped her hand around the base of his cock, squeezing slightly. He thought it wasn't so bad, but then she began to stroke him.

"Is it good?"

He nodded as his eyes rolled back. It felt so different, having someone touch him like this. Or maybe because it was Willa. Gritting his teeth, he let the pleasurable shivers pass over him like waves in the ocean, washing over him until he couldn't think of anything else.

"How about like this?" She changed the pressure and pace.

"Yes ..." He inhaled a sharp breath. "A little faster—oh." He shut his eyes tight and bit at his lip. "Please ... I can't ..."

She released him, then rolled on her back. He wanted to

look into her eyes as they made love, so he covered her body with his and positioned himself between her thighs. "So lovely," he said, staring down at her face. Taking his cock in hand, he pointed it at her wet slit, pushing inside slowly.

"Thoralf," she moaned.

He stopped. "Is that ... okay?"

"Yes," she said with a throaty giggle. "Don't stop." Holding his breath, he pushed in further. "You feel so good."

She felt incredible, but he was too focused on his task to say a word. After what seemed like eternity, he was fully inside her.

He'd always wondered what this moment would be like. His imagination could never live up to what he was feeling now, not just with the physical sensations but the idea of being with Willa in this way.

"Are you all right?" Her teeth sank into her lower lip.

"Better than all right," he assured her, and placed a quick peck on her lips. "Can I ..."

"Oh, yes."

Bracing himself on his elbows, he moved experimentally. She was so hot and tight, and the friction was maddening. He reared back, leaving just his tip inside her and then pushed back in.

"More—oh!" She shivered when he repeated the motion. "Faster."

He rolled forward and back, following her undulations. As they continued, he lost control of his body, the mindless pleasure urging him to keep going. The feel of her, the tightness gripping him, was almost too much, and it was a miracle he managed not to come right away.

Hands grabbed at his buttocks, fingers digging in to push him in deeper. Moving his head down, he kissed her roughly, invading her mouth with his tongue in a rhythm that matched his hips. When she brought her knees up, he plunged in deeper, and she cried out into his mouth as her body shivered.

He drove into her quicker, and his heart pounded so loudly, she could probably feel it thumping. Finally, he broke and released the pressure that was building like a dam. Her sex clenched around him, multiplying the pleasure of his orgasm.

Arms hooked around his neck and brought him down for another kiss and he groaned low into her mouth. Thoralf swore his eyesight turned white. *Heaven*, he thought. *This was heaven.*

"Oh ... Goddess ..." she panted. "That was—"

"Amazing." He kissed her damp brow and then slowly withdrew from her body, then collapsed on the mattress beside her. They lay there, side-by-side, in silence for a few minutes until they both caught their breaths.

"Was that everything you thought it would be?" She moved up to his side and kissed his chest.

"More." He sighed and turned to face her. "You are everything I dreamed of and more." The words came so naturally to him, he didn't even care that they had really only known each other a few days.

"So are you," she replied. "I want to be with you, Thoralf. For as long as we can be together. For as long as you want me."

Part of him wanted to tell her that he could never *not* want her, but he understood what she was saying. "And I want to be with you, for as long as you'll have me." She reached up and cupped his cheek.

Turning his head, he kissed her palm. "Then let's be together." She cuddled closer to him and let out a yawn. "Get some rest," he urged.

The adrenaline rushing through him ebbed away, and his body remembered he was still recovering. So, he closed his eyes and held her close. As he drifted off, he thought he heard something from deep inside him rumbling, but the fog of sleep muffled the faint growl.

CHAPTER 11

Willa couldn't remember the last time she awoke feeling so light and happy. Maybe never. Even in the last few months when she convinced herself she was content with her life, she knew part of it was because she was resigned to her fate. But as soon as she opened her eyes, it was as if she was floating on air, and nothing could bring her down.

A heavy arm landed on her waist. "Are you awake?"

"Yes." She yawned. "You?"

"I've been up for a while."

She twisted around to face him. "Why didn't you wake me up?"

"Because I wanted to watch you sleep." His handsome face lit up. "You look beautiful."

"Thank you." Willa knew she was attractive, but when Thoralf said it, she actually felt beautiful. "How long have we been out?" It was still bright outside, but the sun was much higher now.

"Two or three hours? It's just half past eleven," he said. "I think I heard someone come in and bring food. Are you hungry?"

"Not yet."

"I am," he murmured. "But not for food." His already-hard cock pressed against her buttocks, and he nibbled at her neck, making her instantly wet.

Oh Goddess ...

Spreading her legs, she guided his cock between her folds, sighing as he began to fill her. While initially tensing, her body relaxed as he fully seated inside her. His hands cupped her breasts, twisting the nipples to hardness. To her frustration, his hips remained still, so she rolled her hips.

"Patience." He nipped at her neck. "I love just feeling your body."

"Thoralf, I—oh!" He gave her nipples a pinch, sending a shock of pleasure through her. "Please."

Groaning, he began to move his hips. Small shivers of pleasure intensified as his thrusts became faster and harder. When his hand snaked down between her thighs to pluck at her clit, she quickly exploded in orgasm. "Thoralf!"

She had barely recovered when he pulled out of her. Her body protested, until he lay her flat on her back and slid down between her thighs.

Midnight blue eyes blazed with passion as he looked up at her. "Let me taste you."

She nodded, and he dove in with enthusiasm.

Holy Goddess!

His tongue licked at her, laving her with attention. When he lapped at her clit, her hips jumped off the bed. Looking down at him, watching him devour her was a feast for her eyes. Then those midnight blue orbs locked onto hers as he pressed a finger into her slit. One, then a second finger joined in, thrusting in and out of her and her body shook once more.

Once she regained her senses, she grabbed his shoulders and pulled him up, then hooked her ankles around his hips to roll him around so she wound up on top.

His eyes widened. "Willa."

"My captive," she said cheekily, then slid her hands up from his rock-hard abdomen to his chest. She grinned at him then reached between them to guide him into her. His breath hitched, as she sank down on him. When he lifted his hands up, she quickly wrapped her hands around his wrists and pinned them to the mattress. "Nuh-uh, my captive. I didn't say you could touch me."

"Tease," he muttered, yet that must have turned him on even more as his pupils dilated.

Smirking, she moved her hips back and forth. While this wasn't one of her favorite positions, she found it did have its advantages—namely that she could watch Thoralf's face change as she moved. She particularly loved the way he would bite his lip when she squeezed her inner muscles. Planting her knees down, she changed her motions to move up and down, the drag and friction of his cock inside her sending little shocks up her spine. His hips surged upwards, trying to get her to move more, but she only responded by squeezing him tighter.

He growled. "Stop ... teasing."

For some reason, the dominant command touched something primal in her. Part of her wanted to yield to him, but another wanted him to fight. To work for her.

She tightened her grip on his wrists then put them on either side of his head so she leaned down over him. "Make me." Of course, it didn't take much effort for him to flip their positions, and though she let out an outraged gasp, she absolutely loved it.

Once he pinned her under him, he thrust deep into her, making her cry out. He moved within her, fast, hard, and rough. She clawed down his back, encouraging him, and dug her heels into his buttocks as if he could possibly get deeper in her. The drag of his cock, the weight of his body, and the motion of his hips were too much, and soon, they both tumbled over the edge into orgasm.

When they both returned to earth, Thoralf gathered her into his arms and kissed her softly. "I didn't hurt you, did I?"

Her heart warmed at his concern. "Not at all. It was ... hot."

He let out a breath. "I was worried I was too rough."

"Hmmm, sometimes rough is nice," she assured him. "I like this side of you."

"Really? I wasn't too brutal?"

"I don't want you to be violent or anything. And I do like the way we took things slow and gentle the first time. But I also like it when you don't hold back." She touched his cheek. "I'm not made of glass."

"I know. You're stronger than you look." He kissed her again, then withdrew from her. "You must be hungry. Give me a moment, and I'll bring you some food."

She watched him disappear into the bathroom, then re-emerged to head out to the living area. Heading into the bathroom, she cleaned up and got re-dressed, finishing just in time to see him return with a tray, which he put down on the bed.

"The staff left all this food outside. This is just a selection, and there's more if we're still hungry.

The smell of the food made her stomach rumble in hunger. "It smells and looks amazing."

They had a feast in bed with freshly-baked flat breads, juicy skewered meats, crisp salads. There was also a bottle of wine to wash everything down.

"I've never gone swimming at the beach before," she sighed, staring out at the ocean. The master bedroom featured a patio that had direct access to the beach. A few steps out of the glass doors, and they were at the shore. "I wish we could stay."

He nibbled at her neck. "Who says we can't?"

She chuckled. "This isn't a vacation."

He quirked his eyebrows at her. "It can be."

"Thoralf, we have a lot of work to do," she reminded him. "The book."

"Will be there when return to the Northern Isles." He kissed her lips. "Destroying the lab was a huge victory for our side. Aleksei had been nagging me to take time for myself. I think it's time I take him up on his offer. Would you like to stay here for a while longer?"

Her hand went to her heart. "Can we?"

"I'll arrange it."

Thoralf didn't elaborate further and left her in the villa. He came back half an hour later. "It's done. Aleksei says take all the time we need, and Xander Stavros has welcomed us as his guests for as long as we want. In fact, he invited us to dinner at the main house tonight with his father and Alpha, Ari Stavros."

"Xander Stavros *welcomed* us?" Her jaw nearly unhinged. "Like, he actually said we could stay?"

He nodded, then grinned at her. "He does owe me a debt for saving his life. Though I think that's not the only reason."

"It's not?"

"You intrigue him, I think. And somehow, you gained his respect by not cowering."

"Jealous?" she teased.

A dark, hot look crossed his face, then he slipped an arm around her. "Maybe. But I know you'll be coming home with me tonight." The kiss he gave her was fiercely possessive and hot. He growled into her mouth when she sank her nails into his shoulders. His cock hardened and pressed urgently against her stomach. "I really wanted to take you out for your first swim." His fingers began to unbutton the front of her dress.

Giggling, she disentangled herself from him then pulled the dress over her head, leaving her completely naked. "Who says you can't?" Turning, she raced out of the bedroom and ran toward the patio, laughing as Thoralf came up behind her. He swept her up into his arms and plunged into the ocean. Salty water bubbled around her as a wave crashed over them.

"Do you like it?" he asked as their heads bobbed out of the water.

"No," she said. "I love it."

His face lit up. "Good."

They frolicked in the ocean, laughing, swimming, and diving into the frothy waves. Who knew water could be so warm and relaxing? The sand was so soft and squishy under her toes and the sun felt divine on her face.

"You've never swum in the ocean?" he asked as they bobbed up and down in the water.

"I have, but never in warm waters like this. The only water I've been in was the cold Arctic Ocean just off Fiorska. Dragonlings are taught to swim once our animals manifested." Though the freezing temperatures didn't bother her, it wasn't exactly comfortable or relaxing, but it was a necessity to learn. "Were you taught as a child?"

He chuckled. "I am a Water Dragon; we learn to swim before we walk. In our human and dragon form, we can breathe underwater."

"Truly?" Different kinds of dragons had different abilities, though they kept it to themselves.

"Yes. We cannot fly long distances, but we are quick and efficient in the water."

"I'd like to see that. Can you show me?"

Thoralf's expression turned serious. "Willa, are you sure?"

"Of course." Why wouldn't— "Oh." He never showed her his dragon because it would be a reminder that she had lost hers. *Silly man.* Why would anything about him make her sad? "Please Thoralf?"

"As you wish," he relented, then swam out far into the open sea until his head disappeared under the waves. A few seconds later, something huge shot out of the water like a rocket.

Willa gasped. Thoralf's dragon was covered in blue green scales and had two large horns on top of its head. Its wings were small and bat like, and its tail was fluked like a dolphin's. The creature flew further out, then dove back in the water.

The undercurrent told her something big was heading

her way and sure enough, an enormous head emerged from the water a few inches from her.

"H-hello," she greeted Thoralf's dragon. Its eyes were enormous, but were the same color as Thoralf's.

The creature blinked and snorted.

"Aren't you a handsome one?" Tentatively she reached out. She expected it to recoil, but to her surprise, it stilled as her hand touched its leathery snout.

The dragon let out a sigh and closed its eyes, then nuzzled at her palm.

"Oh, friendly, aren't you?"

It responded by nudging at her arm.

"Do you ... want something?"

The dragon maneuvered its body around to face the open water, then bent its neck at her, pointing at its back with its snout.

"Do you want me to ride you?"

It dipped its head low.

Willa hesitated for a moment. "Oh, why not?" She treaded forward so she was right above the dragon's back. The creature grunted, which for some reason she interpreted as "hold on." Grabbing onto its scales, she pulled herself forward.

She shrieked as the dragon suddenly sped off. Securing her grip, she leaned back and let out a whoop as they skimmed over the water. The wind blew her hair back as the salty water sprayed at her.

It was magnificent.

They continued to race across the azure waters. Sometimes, the water dragon would dive deep, plunging them into the ocean for a few seconds. It would also leap into the air, and for a moment, Willa could fly again.

"Thank you," she said to the dragon and placed a kiss on one of its scales. It replied with a soft roar before heading back to shore. Climbing off its back, she took a few steps back and watched at the beautiful creature began to shrink.

"That was wonderful," she said to Thoralf when he finished shifting back. "Thank you for taking me."

He scratched at his head. "It was more my dragon's idea. But I glad you enjoyed it."

"It was exhilarating." Stepping forward, she moved into the circle of his arms. "Let's go back inside."

They stayed inside all afternoon making love, exploring each other's bodies. She'd never been with anyone quite like Thoralf—eager, responsive, and hungry for her. But she, too, couldn't get enough of him. She loved watching his face twist with pleasure each time he came into her and they pushed each other toward their orgasm.

Sated and spent, she had drifted off to sleep when she heard a knock at the door.

"I'll get it," he offered and dashed out of the bedroom. He returned later with a large white box and a frown on his face.

"What is it?"

"It's for you. From Xander Stavros." He placed it on top of the bed.

"For me?"

"A gift," he added through gritted teeth. "Why would he give you a gift?"

"I don't know." Crawling toward the box, she took the lid off and lifted out the item inside. "A dress?" The silky fabric looked expensive. "Perhaps to wear tonight?"

"We should decline their invitation."

"What? That would be rude. Why—" It was then she noticed the expression on his face. "Oh, come on, Thoralf, you're not jealous, are you?"

His jaw set. "This gift is not appropriate."

She couldn't believe he was jealous. Over Xander Stavros, who'd more likely send her packing from his island than seduce her.

"Thoralf, there's no need to be jealous. You're the only one I want." Taking his hand, she pulled him into bed and showed him just how much she wanted him.

A golf cart came later that evening and drove them up a hill to the magnificent sprawling villa at the top. A butler welcomed them and ushered them inside, past the foyer and into a large living area.

The inside of the villa was even more impressive and tastefully decorated, but it was obvious the people who lived here were wealthy. Everything was white, with touches of gold and splashes of color here and there. The huge windows opened up to the ocean of course, and Willa could only guess the view was fantastic during the daytime.

Willa didn't know much about Aristotle "Ari" Stavros initially, so Thoralf explained that the Alpha was also a billionaire shipping magnate. He also formed The Shifter Protection Agency, or The Agency, whose entire mission was to protect their kind all over the world, filling in where law enforcement or governments could not act.

"Welcome, welcome." A tall silver-haired man dressed in

a tan suit greeted them as they entered what appeared to be the dining area. Xander Stavros stood next to him, and from their resemblance, Willa guessed the older man had to be Ari Stavros.

"Nice to see you again, Thoralf. And you," he began, turning to Willa, "must be Lady Willa." Taking the hand she offered, he kissed it. "Welcome, you honor us with your presence."

"You're too kind, Alpha," she replied. "Thank you for allowing Thoralf to recover in your beautiful home and for having us as guests."

Obviously, Xander Stavros didn't inherit any charm from his father as he merely nodded at them in greeting, his stare imposing as ever.

"My pleasure, now come, let us eat."

Once again, they were treated to some amazing food, and the courses and plates that came in seemed endless. Ari Stavros was friendly and warm, and Willa enjoyed talking to him and listening to him tell them stories, especially about his family. It was obvious he loved his sons and daughters, and he was especially proud of his youngest daughter Cordelia, who was away at university and would be coming home in a few days.

Xander Stavros, on the other hand, was mostly quiet, but his keen dark eyes soaked in everything. She could practically hear the cogs in his brain turning, filing away every piece of information as if to use later.

The night didn't end after dinner as Ari invited them for some dessert and drinks outside on the terrace overlooking the ocean. Xander excused himself, stating that he had business to attend to, so it was just the three of them.

They laughed, drank more wine, and at some point, Ari coaxed them to dance. Music played over the speakers as Ari taught her how to waltz, and after, Thoralf held her in his arms as they swayed to a slow beat, the evening ocean breeze caressing her skin.

"I think it's time for this old man to retire." He winked at them. "And for you young lovers to have your time alone. But stay as long as you like. The driver will bring you back to your villa anytime."

Thoralf's grip tightened around her. "I think we will retire as well. Thank you, Alpha, for your hospitality."

They had barely gotten back into the villa when Thoralf practically ripped off their dress and had her pinned to the wall, growling as he reveled in tearing the fabric to shreds. She sighed in pleasure and perhaps slight disappointment—she really liked that dress and she didn't have anything else to wear. It didn't matter, though, because the next few days, she was barely clothed. When they weren't wrapped up in each other's arms making love, they were swimming in the ocean or simply enjoying each other's company.

Willa hoped it would last forever, but alas, it wasn't meant to be as one morning, they received the call to come back to the Northern Isles. Their return, however, was due to a joyous occasion: Queen Sybil had just given birth to the newest member of the royal family.

CHAPTER 12

After hearing the wonderful news, Willa and Thoralf made plans to go back as soon as possible ,and they left later that day. Since they arrived in the Northern Isles late evening, they decided to first head back to the cottage to spend the night before heading to the palace.

The next morning, Thoralf left to first meet with the king and the rest of the Dragon Guard on official matters, so Willa went to the royal apartments by herself to see the queen and the new baby.

"She's beautiful," Willa said as Queen Sybil presented the small bundle in her arms. The tiny face peeked out from the blanket, her sleepy little eyes blinking as her mouth opened for a yawn. "What's her name?"

"We haven't decided yet," the queen said. "Aleksei and I have a few ideas, but we thought we'd wait a few days. But thank you, I appreciate you coming back right away." The queen flashed her a knowing smile. "I heard you had to cut your vacation short.

Willa blushed. "We needed to come back at some point anyway."

"I'm sure you did." The queen winked at her. "Oh, c'mon, we're adults here. Well, almost all of us." She nodded to the princess. "But she can't understand anything yet. So, Willa ... you and Thoralf, huh?"

The heat in her cheeks intensified. "Yes."

The queen placed the princess back in her crib and pulled her in for a hug. "I'm so happy for you."

Relief rushed through her. "You are?"

"Of course. Why wouldn't I be?"

"Because Thoralf and I aren't fated mates," she said.

While she and Thoralf had agreed to be together despite the fact that they would never form a mate bond, she hadn't thought about what everyone's reactions would be once they left their little bubble in Lykos.

"So? I know lots of couples who aren't mates and stay together. You look so happy and so does he. That's all that matters. And I suppose this means you'll be living here now?"

"I ... yes." Now that she and Thoralf were together, she would make a life wherever he wanted to be.

Queen Sybil let out a rather un-royal squeal. "That's wonderful! Where do you think you'll want to stay? Or what do you want to do?"

"We haven't worked that part out yet." Well, actually they hadn't spoken about any of the details of how their relationship would work. But now that the queen asked ... "I suppose I would need to find a way to earn my keep around here. I can't just keep living off your kindness."

Queen Sybil's face fell. "Oh no, that's not what I was

implying. You're welcome to stay in the cottage for as long as you like."

"I know," she assured the queen. "But I cannot continue living my life cloistered, away from everyone."

Over the last few days with Thoralf, Willa realized something—that she hadn't been truly *living*. She hadn't been content or happy, but rather, she'd been resigned to her fate. Now, she had a chance to make something of herself.

"We can talk it over," the queen said. "Brainstorm some ideas. I'm sure you'll be able to find something to do. You can even go to school if you want."

"I'll think about it." She glanced at the clock. "You should probably get some rest. And I need to go check on what's happening with the diary." She'd been so caught up in Thoralf that she'd nearly forgotten about Ephyselle.

After they said their goodbyes, Willa headed straight toward the library. As soon as she entered the office in the back, Gideon lifted his head from the where he was crouched over a laptop. A knowing smile spread over his face. "Glad to see you back. How was the vacation?"

Thoralf no doubt had told him, and perhaps all of the Dragon Guard, about their relationship. "Wonderful," she said, sauntering over and plopping down on the empty chair beside him. "How are we doing on the translations?"

"I knew you'd ask." Reaching behind him, he grabbed a second laptop and placed it in front of her. "I finished scanning all the pages, and the translations are almost done, just a few more pages left. But it bookmarked all the places where Aristaeum is mentioned."

Excitement pounded in her veins. "Did you find any references to a cure or the temple?"

"I don't know, I haven't read it." Opening the laptop, he tapped a few keys. "Thoralf mentioned this meant a lot to you." He got up and retrieved the book from the scanner and handed it to her. "So, I thought maybe you'd like to read it first."

Hugging the book to her chest, she nodded. "Thank you." *Leave it to Thoralf to be so thoughtful.*

Turning to the laptop, she began to read through the translated passages. While she was tempted to know more about the Ephyselle and her life, she had to focus on the search for the cure. After all, now that the grunt work was done, she could read the diary at her leisure. She opened the bookmarked passages and clicked on the first mention of Aristaeum.

I have received word that my tribe's old enemy, the vile Wizard Aristaeum, is up to his old tricks. A messenger arrived from my old village with a letter from my old teacher, Guiselda. The Goddess has spoken to her in a dream, and since then, she could feel the magic changing in the air.

The Wizard is planning something big.

She skipped to the next bookmark.

Guiselda's spies have returned from their long trek to Aristaeum's mountain hideaway. They described the most heinous things happening there. He has captured other animal-skin walkers. Then he somehow removed their animal skins, leaving them vulnerable and weak.

She gasped. That was definitely the work of The Wand.

News has spread of the slaughter of an entire tribe of animal-skin walkers. Gustav sent one of his men to investigate, and when he came back, he told us that two dozen people—men, women and children—were found murdered, seemingly rounded up and had their throats slit, unable to defend themselves from their attackers nor heal from their wounds.

They had just been left there to die.

Tears gathered at the corner of her eyes. *Those poor people.* Taking a deep breath, she continued to the next bookmark.

We have confirmed that Aristaeum and his minions, indeed, have created some kind of weapon that removes an animal-skin walker's ability to change into their creature form. According to our spies, Aristaeum had found an ancient magical object that could temporarily entrap an animal skin-walker's creature. However, using his own power, he built a better one, a scepter that could completely separate the creature from its human host.

Guiselda and I have been poring all over the ancient texts, and I think we are getting closer to finding a way to reverse the scepter's effects. If our suspicions are correct, the wizard is using some ancient form of transference magic. To create such a powerful object requires a lot of magical energy, and this energy cannot simply be created. It must be taken from one source and given to another.

I shudder to think how Aristaeum was able to do this and the source of the magic. But then again, his followers are many, and their blind allegiance to their leader could cause them to do anything for him.

Whatever this transference magic was, it didn't sound good. Willa didn't know for sure, but it sounded like to create The Wand, Aristaeum had to drain his followers' magic. In the following bookmarked passages, Ephyselle wrote of her research into the magic scepter, as well as several attempts to counteract its magic, but all of them failed. Willa looked at the list of bookmarks and saw that there was one left.

It has taken several cycles, but I have finally found the solution. The spell can be broken and the animal-skin walkers reunited with their creature. Guiselda, myself, and several of our allies have gathered in the temple to the Goddess in the mines of Harvgit.

Using the same kind of magic the vile Wizard used, we have transferred our own powers to the Altar of the Goddess.

Mines of Harvgit ...

Every hair on Willa's body stood on end as a memory flooded back into her brain. Could it be ...?

I thought it had been a dream.

She needed to find out more, so she kept on reading.

As we speak, Gustav has rallied his and his allies' forces to steal the scepter and bring it here. The scepter must be destroyed on the altar, for only here, under the eye of the Goddess, can we break the magic's hold.

My magic is spent, but ...

She stopped reading, as the translation hadn't been completed, but she had gathered enough information.

Blood pounded in her ears. This was it. The cure wasn't a potion or a spell. *Only magic can defeat magic*. The same kind of magic, canceling each other out.

"Gideon!" She spun the chair around. "Call everyone. *Now*."

CHAPTER 13

"Excellent job on finally ridding the world of that vile potion," Aleksei said as soon as Thoralf finished giving his report of what happened. They—along with Stein, Niklas, and Rorik—gathered in the king's office for a debrief.

"Thank Thor," Niklas added. "That stuff was awful." A few months ago, he'd been the recipient of the formula and nearly died after the Knights stabbed him.

"We destroyed the lab where they were experimenting and making the formula," Thoralf said. "But there may be some more out there."

But we've ensured they won't be able to make anymore, right? Stein asked. He, too, had been a recipient of the formula.

"Yes. According to The Agency's intelligence, the Knights found a way to use the second wand to synthesize the Formula X-87 and its previous versions. Their scientists are still attempting to figure out how, but at least we've secured the second wand and Xander Stavros is keeping it in a secret location."

Rorik stroked his ruddy beard. "Hopefully there aren't any other wands out there."

"We cannot be certain, but with all the work Gideon and I have put into researching and investigating, we would have found evidence of other wands," Thoralf pointed out.

"We must stay vigilant against any threats, but for now, we must celebrate this major win." Aleksei patted him on the back. "Not to mention, you have returned to us safely."

"Thanks to Stein. I owe you, my friend for fishing me out of the sea."

The stony-faced Dragon Guard didn't reply, but nodded in acknowledgment.

The king stood up and circled around his desk to face Thoralf, then placed a hand on his shoulder. "And you have other good news for us, I suppose?"

"Good news?"

Aleksei laughed. "Come now, Thoralf. We all know the reason you asked for a few days off in Lykos. And who you spent all that time with."

"Your face is as red as a fire engine," Niklas snickered. "Spill, man."

"I ..." Thoralf didn't quite know what to say. On one hand, Aleksei was like a brother to him, and the other men in the room were his closest compatriots. He trusted them wholeheartedly. On the other, what happened between him and Willa was a private matter.

"We do not need details," Aleksei assured him.

We just want to know if you're officially together.

Every pair of eyes in the room zeroed in on Stein.

He shrugged. *Vera's dying to know. She has some kind of bet with the queen. She keeps hounding me about it.*

Thoralf mentally shook his head. "I suppose you could say, yes, we are 'officially' together." Whatever that meant, they hadn't fully discussed, but what they felt for each other didn't need labels.

"That is wonderful news." Aleksei pulled him in for a hug.

"Thank you, Aleksei, everyone. And I know she is not my fated mate, but she is the one that I want, and for some reason only the gods know, she has chosen me."

"So?" Rorik said. "It makes no difference, especially if you make each other happy. We would never judge you or her for your decisions."

"Did you think we would react negatively?" Aleksei asked.

"I have heard all of you say that the mating bond is a special thing," Thoralf added.

"True, but that's not guaranteed with mates either," Niklas said.

He frowned. "It's not?"

"No. Mates could even confess their love to each other, but it still might not form. That's what happened with me and Annika at first. Turns out, I still had issues to work out."

Stein let out a grunt. *And the longer you are together and the bond doesn't form because of a block, the more your animal resents you.*

"See, mating is not the end all and be all. Thoralf, if you love her, that's all that matters," Aleksei added. "The two of you found and have chosen each other, without any help from your animals. That does not mean yours is a lesser love."

"Love?" Thoralf's heart stuttered. He hadn't said the words aloud yet, but—

"Are you just discovering now that you are in love with her?" Aleksei's eyes twinkled in mirth as he clucked his tongue. "Of course you are."

"H-how did you guess?"

"I know you, my friend. My brother." Then he added silently, and only to him, *and after all the waiting, I knew you would only be with a woman you truly cared about.*

Niklas raised a fist in the air. "We should celebrate! Maybe have an official party for Lady Willa to welcome her into the fold."

Before anyone else could answer, however, Gideon's voice rang through their mind link.

You must all come to the library. Willa's found something in the book.

All five men looked at each other, and without another word, they filed out of the office and headed to the library.

Once they arrived, Thoralf was by Willa's side instantly. "Willa, what's wrong? Gideon said you'd explain. Did you find something in the diary?"

Her eyes sparkled as she grinned up at him. "Yes," she said, then relayed everything she read from the translations.

"That is amazing news," Aleksei said. "But where is the temple? Do the mines still exist?"

Willa shook her head. "I'm afraid not, Your Majesty. But they are not lost, the mine simply ran out and abandoned. After a few years, the Alpha—my grandfather—built our compound over it. He had intended to use the tunnels in the mine as some kind of underground city or escape route, but it just never happened. My father said he remembers all the construction, but then they just stopped. Then, one day when I was a child, something strange happened.

"I was playing in the main hall by myself and found this door on the southwest corner. I pushed on it, and then it just opened up and I stepped inside. I remember this long, dark hallway. It was cold, so cold, even for me. I heard some strange sounds and ran away and the door closed behind me. When I went to my father and told him about the door, he became angry and told me never to go near the door again. I didn't tell him I went inside, though."

"Not even when you grew up?" Thoralf asked.

"I forgot about it. But now that I've read through the diary, I have this feeling it might be connected. Perhaps my grandfather sensed the magic when he was trying to build over the mines, or somehow, Ephyselle used a spell to ward off anyone trying to access the temple."

"It's possible." The king thought for a moment. "So far, what the diary has told us matches what we know of the wands. It's worth trying to find it so we can quickly destroy The Wand and reverse its effect. Rorik, retrieve The Wand as soon as possible. Thoralf, you and Lady Willa prepare to leave for Fiorska. You can take Rorik and Ranulf with you this time."

Willa tensed beside him. Reaching out to take her hand, he squeezed it tight. "You do not have to go, if you don't want to. Right, Your Majesty?"

"Of course," Aleksei replied. "Forgive me for being insensitive, Lady Willa. You do not have to return to Fiorska if it is too painful."

Her lower lip trembled. "I don't want to be apart from you, Thoralf. Look what happened the last time."

He could see the conflict on her face. While he appreciated her concern, he didn't want her hurt by the memories of the place where she had lost everything. "That's different." He kissed her knuckles. "We were on a dangerous mission into enemy territory. Now, we are simply going to a deserted place to destroy The Wand on top of the altar. Nothing will happen to me. I will be back before you know it. And who knows? If this does work, then you'll welcome me back by greeting my dragon with yours."

"I ... I will. I have faith in you, Thoralf. You'll finish your mission and restore your honor."

Had he forgotten that was what he set out to do initially? After everything that happened with Willa, his honor became low priority. "Thank you for your faith."

"We must leave at once," Rorik said. "I will inform my father, and he can meet us before we leave for Fiorska." After securing The Wand after the attack, they had entrusted it to Niels, Rorik's father and a former Captain of the Dragon Guard, for safekeeping.

Thoralf rubbed his chin with his thumb and forefinger. "So, we must destroy The Wand on the Altar of the Goddess. What else can you tell us about this passageway?"

She bit her lip and narrowed her eyes. "There are columns running along that wall. The door is between the third and fourth one, nearly invisible because of the pattern of the design carved into the wall. Now that I think about it, it was almost as if it were done deliberately."

"I think we have enough information to destroy The Wand," Rorik said. "Thoralf is right, there is no need for Lady Willa to come with us."

"See?" He kissed her temple. "We will be back before

you know it." He then turned to the others. "I will meet you outside on the main lawn in fifteen minutes. I need a moment alone with Willa before we leave." *There is something I must do before we leave*, he told everyone through their mind link.

Aleksei looked at him knowingly. *I'm happy for you, Thoralf.* Clearing his throat, he turned to the rest of the Dragon Guard. "Let's give Thoralf and Lady Willa some privacy."

Once they were alone, Thoralf scrounged up his courage. "Willa, there's—"

"Thoralf, can you—" she said at the same time. "Sorry, go ahead."

"No, you go first."

"Are you sure I can stay?" Willa asked, her expression uncertain. "You're right, it can't be dangerous."

"I do not fear for our safety." Thoralf wrapped her hands in his. "But your well-being is my number one priority. I want to save you the heartache of reliving the past. Besides, we already know what to do. There's no need for you to be there."

"I suppose you're right." Her teeth sank into her lower lip. "So, what did you want to say to me?"

"Ah, yes." Thoralf's throat suddenly turned dry. "I—" His voice croaked like bullfrog's, so he swallowed, hoping to moisten his vocal cords.

"Thoralf?" She turned her head. "What's wrong?"

"Nothing. I just ..."

Those ice blue eyes gazed up at him, and her lovely face mesmerized him.

Odin, give me strength.

"Willa, I just wanted to tell you ..."

His heart pounded so loud, it drowned out every sound.

Just say it!

"Thoralf?"

"*Willaaliveyew.*"

"I beg your pardon?" Her brows scrunched up. "Did you say 'alive yew'?"

"I love you," he burst out. "I just ... thought you should know."

She stared at him for the longest time, not speaking, not moving.

Thoralf's stomach dropped. "You do not feel the same way."

"What?" She blinked. "No! I mean, of course I do!" She jumped up and wrapped her arms around his neck. "I love you too, you silly goose!"

Thoralf's heart leapt into his throat. "Willa ..." He kissed her deep, as if sending every feeling and emotion he could muster to her. She responded eagerly, passionately, and he had no doubts of her love.

"I wish we had more time," he murmured when they broke away.

"We will, when you return." She smiled brightly at him. "Be safe," she urged. "And come back to me."

"You know I will."

CHAPTER 14

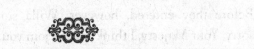

Coward.

The words rang in Willa's head over and over again as she watched the four dragons depart, flying high above them, growing smaller and smaller until they all but disappeared.

"They will be fine," King Aleksei assured her. "And will be back before you know it."

She believed him. At least, she believed the king believed his own words. "I'm sure you're right." *But I'm still a coward for not joining them.*

"And they have an extra pair of hands and eyes. Neils was one of the best Dragon Guard captains before he retired, that's why I chose to give him The Wand for safekeeping."

When the older Dragon Guard arrived, Thoralf had explained to her that he was Rorik's father and a former captain. It had been an unconventional choice to have him hide The Wand, but one that their enemies would not expect should they attempt to retrieve it.

The king gestured back to the palace. "Now, let's go back

inside. I think Sybil should be feeling rested enough for visitors. She would surely love to see you again, and you can join us for lunch."

"I'm sure you're eager to go back to Her Majesty and the princess," she said.

The king's face lit up. "Indeed, I am."

They headed back inside toward the royal apartments. Before they entered, however, Willa stopped short. "I'm sorry, Your Majesty, I think I won't join you."

"No?"

Her hands clenched into fists. "I just have this feeling."

It was difficult to explain exactly why she felt this way. Maybe because things were different now, as if exchanging those three little words with Thoralf earlier today had shifted her entire world. *I didn't even say it to him again before he left.*

"You are distressed because Thoralf has left. I understand. But why not distract yourself for the afternoon?"

"It's not that." There was a foreboding building up in her chest. "I should have gone with them."

"No, Thoralf was correct." King Aleksei patted her shoulder gently. "I should not have asked you to go in the first place. I was there, you know, that day when we found you ... Even I sometimes have nightmares about what I saw, and I cannot even begin to imagine how you must feel. Sending you there would no doubt traumatize you, and Thoralf would never forgive me or himself for causing you pain."

"It was so long ago, but the pain feels so fresh." Even now, the grief hit her hard. "Your Majesty, if you'll excuse me, I just need some time alone."

"As you wish, but I'm sure Sybil would welcome you anytime."

"Give her my regards and tell her I'll come visit tomorrow."

Willa thought of going back to the cottage, but then there was nothing for her to do there except wait and be reminded of Thoralf's absence. An idea popped into her head. *I should finish reading Ephyselle's diaries.* She skipped over all the parts that didn't pertain to Aristaeum after all, and Gideon said they were nearly done.

She headed to the library, making her way to the back room. Gideon was there, but to her surprise, he wasn't alone. There was a blonde woman sitting on the chair where Willa had previously occupied, working on a laptop.

"Lady Willa, hello" Gideon greeted. "What are you doing here?"

The blonde woman looked up. "Hello." Silvery blue eyes stared back at her, and Willa instantly knew what she was. *Dragon.*

"Um, I didn't know you had c-company," she stammered. "I was hoping to read the rest of the translations, but I can come back—"

The woman stood up. "No, I can leave." She was tall and athletic, her wild blonde hair tamed into braids against her scalp. There was an intimidating vibe around her that filled the room, and Willa could tell she was not one to be messed with.

"You don't have to," Willa said. "Please, you were here first."

"There's plenty of space for you both," Gideon said. "Lady Willa, have you met Annika?"

"Not formally, no. Nice to meet you, Annika."

"Lady Willa." She gave her a slow nod. "I'm glad to finally be introduced to you. You're all my daughter talks about these days."

"Daughter—oh, right." The children from the picnic. "Maya. She's precious, as are the rest of your kids."

"I hope they did not disturb your peace."

"Not at all, I was happy to meet them."

Gideon cleared his throat. "Did you say you wanted to read the rest of the translation, Lady Willa?"

"If possible." She glanced at the laptop Annika had been working on. "I can come back—"

"No, I have them backed up, let me load it up for you." Gideon rooted around his desk. "I just ... oh here you go." He handed her the laptop. "Listen, I need to go start my shift, but you already know how to work the program. Stay as long as you like." He bid them both goodbye and left the room.

"You are reading the translations for the book that mentions the cure for The Wand, correct?" Annika asked.

She sat down across from Annika. "Yes."

"I'm reading some translations as well. Of my father's diaries. Gideon created this computer program to translate the old Northern Isles language since no one could understand them."

Willa sat down. "Oh, how interesting. He never taught you?"

She shook her head. "He died before he could."

Her hand froze halfway as she opened the laptop. "I'm sorry. My father died too, a few years ago."

"I ... have heard." Annika glanced around. "I'm sorry. My mate told me the story. I've been living here for a few months now and never knew you were here. When we came to your cottage the other day, he had no choice but to tell me."

"I hope you weren't too mad that he had to keep me a secret."

"Not at all. I understand the duty of the Dragon Guard. My father had been one too, before he died."

"How long ago did he die?"

"Not long, less than a year ago." Grief struck her face. "Does it get better?"

Willa had to contemplate her words. She wished she could give Annika some reassurance. "It's been three years since my father passed. At first, it was all I could think of. The pain, it's like ..." She grasped for a way to explain it. "Think of a bouncing ball inside a box with a button. Each time the ball hits the button, you remember your loss and it hurts. In the beginning, that ball seems massive. Like every little thing will remind you of him and it hits that button all the time. Again and again. You can't get rid of the button or take the ball out of the box. But after a while, that ball gets smaller and it doesn't hit the button as often. But when it does—"

"The pain comes back," Annika finished. "I think, I understand. My ball is still big."

"Exactly. But don't worry, over time, you will find a way to manage it." Her throat tightened.

"My father died by the hands of our enemies, The Knights of Aristaeum," Annika said. "As did yours."

Willa met her silvery blue gaze. "I'm sorry."

"We will make them pay."

"I know we will." She turned the laptop on, and the screen blinked. "I should get back to reading."

"As will I."

She waited for the program to start running and then went to last page she read before she left for Lykos. As she always did when she read Ephyselle's words, a strange feeling washed over her, like she was somehow intimately connected to this woman who had lived so long ago.

She read for what seemed like a long time, becoming totally engrossed in Ephyselle's daily life when a beeping sound from the laptop interrupted her, and the program froze.

"What ... oh no!" She tapped on the buttons, but nothing happened.

"Are you all right?" Annika asked.

"I ... something's happening to the program." Her heart sank. "I-I think I broke it."

The female dragon got up from her chair and circled around the table. "Do not worry, Lady Willa." Turning the computer toward her, Annika tapped on a few keys, and the screen unfroze. "See? The program simply finished the translation."

"It did?" She looked at the screen, and sure enough, it jumped a few pages ahead. "Gideon said it was almost done."

"Turning it on must have re-activated it."

"Right. Huh." Squinting at the screen, she saw that it went to the last bookmarked page she had read, the one where Ephyselle spoke of the temple. To her surprise, a few sentences were added on.

The scepter must be destroyed on the altar, for only here, under the eye of the Goddess, can we break the magic's hold.

My magic is spent, but blood is more powerful. I have instructed my daughter, Linnea, to destroy the scepter.

Only she has the ability to reverse the Wizard's magic as my blood runs through her. She must lay scepter on the altar of the Goddess and destroy it.

Blood is more powerful.

Only she has the ability.

Willa sucked in a deep breath. "It's not going to work."

Annika frowned. "What is wrong?"

"They won't be able to destroy The Wand." Her heart pounded in her chest.

"Why not? Was the translation wrong?"

"No, not at all." A laugh bubbled within her. How could she have been so blind? All this time, she knew why she felt so connected to this book. To Ephyselle. "But they will fail." She showed Annika the last part of the translation.

"I see. Should we tell the king so he may recall Thoralf and his team?"

"There's no need."

"But the book says they won't be able to do anything."

"No, they won't. But I can." The moment she said it,

admitted what she knew her heart was telling her, it became so clear. "I'm of her blood. I was descended from Ephyselle."

"You are certain?"

"Yes. Her mate was the Alpha. Only the eldest son or daughter of the Alpha may rule, and according to my father, we can trace our lineage back to the very first Ice Dragon Alpha in Fiorska. So, you see, Ephyselle must be my ancestor, and her blood runs through me."

"What do we do? Should we call them?"

"I'm afraid we can't do that," she said. "We don't have cell towers in Fiorska. I think we may have used satellite communication, but those probably are no longer in operation since no one's been maintaining them. There are also backup communication towers, but that's only for calling outside."

"Then we must go after them."

"Go after them?" She cocked her head to the side. "What do you mean?"

"I can take you, my lady," Annika said. "We can save a trip and be rid of that vile object once and for all."

Her chest tightened and she flinched instinctively. How could she forget that in order for her to destroy The Wand on the altar, she had to go back to Fiorska? "I ... we don't have to go so soon, right? Perhaps we could wait a while. I could be wrong. Maybe Ephyselle is not my ancestor."

"Do not do this."

Her head whipped toward the female dragon. "Do what?"

"Let your fear and pain hold you back. It's blocking what you know in your heart to be true." Annika gripped her shoulders. "Lady Willa, you must take control of the ball ... or the button. Work through the pain, for the sake of the greater good. If my father was anything like yours, then he would have wanted that."

"I ..." The tightness in her chest eased. "You're right, Annika. I can't run away from this forever. I must face my pain."

"Good." Annika straightened her shoulders.

"Will we be able to catch them in time? What if we miss them?" She checked the clock. "According to the plan, they should be halfway to Fiorska by now."

"Do not worry, my lady. I am an Air Dragon. I can fly much faster, and we can make up the time."

"Air Dragon?" She knew of them, of course, and had even met their Alpha, Matthias Thorne. "I thought you said your father was a Dragon Guard?"

"It's a long story, perhaps I will tell you once this is all done."

Willa smiled warmly at the female dragon. "I would like that."

CHAPTER 15

The journey to Fiorska was long and arduous, and Thoralf couldn't help but feel a sense of dread on their way there. He wasn't sure how to describe it; like an itch that wouldn't go away or that he couldn't reach. Maybe he just didn't like leaving Willa, but he knew she couldn't be here. It would cause her too much pain and that he couldn't bear. *I just need to get this done and everything will be all right*. But still ...

"Are you all right?" Niels asked when they landed just outside the former compound of the Ice Dragons.

Thoralf rubbed his chin with this thumb and forefinger. "I'm not sure." He felt inside his inner jacket pocket for The Wand as if reassuring himself that it was still there. It felt strange to be holding it after all this time. But hopefully, after today, the cursed thing would cease to exist.

"Holy Heimdall," Ranulf exclaimed. "I've never seen anything like this."

Thoralf glanced up at the building in front of them. Surprisingly, it looked the same as it did when he first came here three years ago. The white, imposing structure hadn't changed at all, at least on the outside. But then again, it was made to withstand the harsh cold of the arctic.

"You look perturbed," the former Dragon Guard said. "Tell me what's going on."

"I don't know why, but my gut says there's something not quite right."

Rorik frowned. "You should always trust your instinct."

"Ah, right you are, my son," Neils added. "What do you want to do?"

Thoralf thought for a moment. "Ranulf, I want you to fly up and keep watch. Not too far that you can't reach us through our mind link, but high enough that you can spot anything approaching."

"What am I looking for?" the young Dragon Guard asked.

"I don't know. Report anything unusual."

"Will do." Ranulf quickly shifted back into his dragon form and took to the skies.

"All right, let's head inside."

Thoralf led Rorik and Neils into the compound, going past the first gate and then into the main building.

"I thought it would be dark in here," Neils commented.

"It's all the windows," Thoralf pointed out.. "And time of year."

"The midnight sun," Rorik finished. "The lights still work, too, and the temperature is actually comfortable."

"Geothermal power." Thoralf nodded at the vents on the floor. "This place was built to last forever. Prince Harald didn't want it disturbed in any way, so we just left it as is. The systems are automated and require little maintenance, which makes sense because of the lack of manpower."

As they entered the main hall, that dread came back to Thoralf, but this time because of the memories this place held. He would never forget the sight of all those people on the ground, lying down motionless. And then finding Willa ...

He blocked out the images in his head. There was no need to think of that now that they were here, and soon, they would reverse The Wand's effects.

"Where's this sealed door again?" Rorik asked.

"Southwest corner of the main hall." Thoralf led them through the maze-like corridors of the building until they reached the center where the main hall was located. He pointed to one of the corners. "It should be over there."

The three men walked over to the wall, right between the third and fourth column. Though it was faint and well-hidden, sure enough, there was a door-sized outline on the wall.

Neils placed his palm in the center of it. "How do we open it?"

"Willa said she just pushed on it."

The older dragon placed his other hand on the wall and gave it a push. It slid to the side and opened up.

"It is true then," Rorik gasped. "The temple is here."

"Let's go inside."

Thoralf went in first, shivering as a stiff breeze blew past him.

"*Brrr* ..." Neils rubbed his hands on his arms. "I've never felt such frigid air."

Rorik nodded. "It's just as Lady Willa described."

They continued to walk through the tunnel until Thoralf

saw the light at the end. Soon, they walked into a large, open cavern.

"Amazing," Neils declared. "I've never seen anything like it."

The entire cavern seemed to be made up of ice, which allowed the sun to shine through and bathed everything in a faint blue light.

Rorik looked around. "This must be the temple."

"I think we're underneath a glacial cave," Thoralf guessed. "But where—*there*." Sure enough, on the other end of the temple was an altar that looked to be entirely made of ice. Behind it was what looked like a giant statue of a female figure, looking down. *The Goddess Herself.*

"Let's—"

I just saw some people following you inside. A dozen or so.

Ranulf's voice rang loudly in his head. *Here? Who?*

I don't know, but they have weapons. Guns.

Thoralf's stomach drop. *It must be the Knights.* Who else could it be?

"Our enemies are here?" Rorik exclaimed. "How?"

"Perhaps they've been keeping watch on our movements in and out of the Northern Isles." Thoralf kicked himself. They should have been more careful. "Anyway, that doesn't matter. We can't let the Knights get their hands on The Wand again."

Neils grit his teeth. "They will not."

Thoralf nodded in agreement. *Ranulf, go back to the Northern Isles and get help.*

But I can't leave you—

We can fight them, he roared. After all, they were three dragons against a dozen humans. However, if the Knights were prepared, things could still go south. *If anything happens to us, you are our best chance of being rescued.*

Neils tensed. "What do we—ow!"

"Father?" Rorik caught Neils as he doubled over. "What's the matter? *Yeow—Mother Frigga*!" He slapped the back of his neck. "It's like something bit me—" He let out a growl and then fell to his knees. Both men landed on the floor with a heavy thud.

Thoralf dashed toward them but stopped short when several figures entered the main hall, all brandishing automatic rifles pointed at them.

What in Freya's name ...?

The men moved so silently, which was why none of them heard anyone following from behind. Judging from their padded shoes and full body snowsuits, they were probably wearing special noise-dampening equipment.

"Dragon Guard, we finally meet."

Slowly, Thoralf turned to the source of the voice. Standing in the mouth of the passageway was a tall, imposing man with silvery white hair and a menacing stare. The nostrils of his hooked nose flared as their gazes met.

"Don't even think of shifting. One move and your friends are dead."

"Who are you?" Thoralf asked. "And what are you doing here?"

"I thought it would be obvious by now," he sneered. "I am Lord Harken, Master of the Knights of Aristaeum and heir to the Wizard himself."

So, this was Lord Harken. It had been a long time since he'd heard that name. Aleksei's cousin, Erik, had betrayed them by giving the Knights all the intel they needed to assassinate Prince Harald and launch their attack. Apparently, he'd been approached by their leader, Lord Harken, who'd promised him the throne if he gave them the information.

"What do you want?"

"What else? The Wand."

"I don't have it."

"Liar!" Harken strode toward him. "I can feel The Wand's power. I'd know its whereabouts anywhere in the world." He laughed. "The moment it left the protective magic of the Northern Isles, it called to me. Whispered to me, telling me that it wanted to be free. I've been waiting three long years! Now, hand it to me or my men will kill your friends while they are still under the influence of Formula X-87."

Thoralf gritted his teeth. "Why didn't you just shoot me with the formula and take it from me?"

"Why do you think? Your stupid operation on our lab destroyed all our stock." His eyes gleamed. "And well, as revenge, I wanted to use The Wand on you and make you die a slow, terrible death."

Thoralf weighed his choices. Harken had no idea what this place was. He could make a run for it and destroy The Wand on the altar. However, his friends would be left vulnerable, and Harken could kill them out of spite, plus he'd be trapped inside the temple.

"I am growing impatient, Dragon Guard. Give me The Wand now or suffer the consequences."

I'm going to die either way. His thoughts immediately drifted to Willa. *I love you. I wish I could have said it more than once.*

His dragon scratched at him, as if telling him not to give up. But how was he going to get out of this situation alive?

Seeing as he had no choice, Thoralf reached into his jacket and handed The Wand over to Harken.

"See, that wasn't so hard, was it?" Harken's lips twisted into a cruel smile. "Finally, you are back where you belong." His eyes practically devoured The Wand, lifting it high up before pointing it at Thoralf. "And you ... you will get what you deserve."

Thoralf closed his eyes and braced himself.

CHAPTER 16

After conferring with King Aleksei, he agreed to let them go after Thoralf's team. "Be careful," he said to them. "And good luck."

"Thank you, Your Majesty."

Flying with Annika was the fastest way to catch up with the others, so Willa reluctantly agreed to ride the female dragon. Annika already had some kind of belt harness made for her dragon that could carry humans. It was surprisingly comfortable, and Willa found she didn't mind being flown at all.

Maybe in a few hours, I would be doing my own flying.

The anticipation and excitement made her giddy. She closed her eyes, dreaming of the moment. According to Ephyselle, she only had to put The Wand on the altar to destroy it. But she had to be the one to do it. The power of Ephyselle's blood ran through her veins.

The female dragon let out a shriek.

She patted its pearly white scales. She'd never seen such

a beautiful sight as Annika in her dragon form. It was smaller than a water dragon, with a lizard-like body and massive wings tipped with feathers. And just as Annika said, the dragon was *fast*. It darted through the air like a rocket. In fact, it was as if the air currents around them were pushing them forward for extra speed.

The sea seemed endless underneath them. Willa wasn't sure how much time had passed, but her limbs were starting to ache. Finally, she spotted land in the distance. There.

Fiorska.

It had been her home for all her life. Where she was born and grew up. Now, she wasn't sure what it was to her anymore. Or if she even had a home.

The Air Dragon must have seen it too. Willa didn't think it was possible but they flew even faster. Before they reached land, she spotted something in the distance coming toward them. The dot grew larger as it came closer, until finally she could make out its shape. It was a Water Dragon, but definitely not Thoralf's, as its scales were bright blue instead of blue-green. But why was it coming at them?

The Air Dragon slowed down as the Water Dragon came closer. Its massive wings flapped as they hovered in the air, the other dragon speeding toward them. The long, scaly creature circled around them a few times, then the two creatures drifted westward together.

"We're going the wrong way!" But it was no use as her voice was lost to the wind.

Why were they heading away from Fiorska? She wiggled in the harness and tapped on the Air Dragon's chest, but it ignored her. Slumping back, she waited until the two dragons landed on a nearby inlet.

"What's going on?" she demanded as the two dragons shrank back to human form. She recognized the other one as Ranulf. "Where's Thoralf and the others?"

Dark eyes darted to Annika, and then back to her. "Forgive me, my lady ... but Thoralf and the others were captured."

Willa's heart dropped. "C-captured? By whom?"

"The Knights." His jaw hardened. "When we arrived in Fiorska, Thoralf asked me to stay behind and keep watch. I flew overhead and spotted them coming into the compound, but I was too late to stop them. Thoralf told me to run and get help instead. I think ... I think the Knights took ahold of The Wand."

"No!" Willa cried. "We must get to them."

"Thoralf said to go back to the Northern Isles to get help—"

"That will take too much time." It might already be too late, but Willa knew they had to try.

"We have surprise on our side," Annika said. "We might be able to take them. Or at least get a read on the situation and act accordingly."

"If there's too many of them, we can call for help," Willa added. "There's a communication tower about twenty miles from here. We can reach it in no time if we need to."

"I suppose that's a better plan than swimming all the way back to the Northern Isles," Ranulf relented. "My lady, you should stay here."

"No, I can't. I need to be there."

"But—"

"We need her there to destroy The Wand. I'll explain later," Annika said. "This might be our only chance. Once the Knights have it back and they leave, we may never see The Wand again."

"What do we do then?" the Dragon Guard asked.

"We sneak inside and assess the situation," Willa said. "You can reach out to Thoralf and the others and tell them we are here. There's a chance you won't be able to reach them via your mind link if they've already used The Wand on them." *Or worse.* "In that case, we must steal The Wand before they get away and I can destroy it."

"We must leave now," Annika said, her voice urgent.

They quickly flew off, this time, Cloaking themselves. When they arrived outside the compound, Annika kept her grip on Willa's arm to ensure she remained invisible. Thankfully, there were no guards outside.

"I can't hear any of them," Ranulf whispered, his expression faltering. "I'm so sorry ..."

Annika's lips pulled back. "That doesn't mean they are dead."

Ranulf glanced down at the ground. "I don't see any tracks. And I can hear people inside. They're still in there."

"We can still go in and rescue them, then Lady Willa can reverse The Wand's effects." The female dragon paused for a moment. "Willa, we must remain silent when we go in. Ranulf and I can communicate through our mind link, but you must follow my lead. From here on in, things will go fast, but as soon as you get The Wand, head to the altar and destroy it."

Willa nodded, then lead them all the way into the main hall and toward the southwest corner. Sure enough, there was an open doorway there, but it was guarded by two men in white combat gear. Annika nodded to Ranulf, who dashed forward and knocked the two men unconscious.

Annika dragged her into the open doorway, and down the passageway. This was definitely the same place she had discovered as a child, but there was no time to dawdle and reminisce. They followed the light up ahead, and sure enough, it led to a humungous ice cavern. Willa tried to keep going, but Annika held her in a tight grip and gave her a warning glare. They stopped right at the mouth of the cave, watching the events unfold in front of them.

The three Dragon Guards were piled into a heap in the center of the cavern, surrounded by several men in white combat gear, their guns ready to shoot. A tall man stood off to the side, The Wand in his hand.

"What do you want us to do, Lord Harken?" one of them asked.

"Kill the first two before the formula wears off," he ordered. "As for the other one, secure him. We will take him with us to our new lab. Perhaps our scientists will find a use for a *human* subject."

Willa's throat constricted. *No!* Thoralf's dragon was gone now too. She looked at Annika with pleading eyes, begging for them to do something. Annika nodded and relaxed her grip. This was it. She had to do this. For Thoralf.

"Lord Harken!" One of the men shouted. "The guards we posted outside aren't responding."

"What?" Harken's expression changed from surprise to fury. "They're here!" He glanced around, eyes crazed. "Use your infrared goggles now!"

Mother Goddess!

Annika and Ranulf looked at each other, clearly caught by surprise. While Cloaking magic allowed dragons to hide from human sight, infrared picked up heat so they would surely be discovered.

"There!" One of the men shouted, pointing their gun in their direction. "I can see them! Three targets, your three o'clock, Lord Harken!"

Harken's face twisted in fury, and he pointed The Wand toward them.

"Now!" Annika shouted, releasing Willa before she leapt out of the way.

Adrenaline pumped through her veins and she surged forward. As she no longer had an animal to lose, The Wand had no effect on her, and the beam of light emanating from it simply passed through her. Harken screamed as Willa tackled him to the ground. She reached out and grabbed The Wand from his hand then rolled off him, quickly getting to her feet.

"Destroy it!" Annika shouted as Ranulf shifted into his dragon form, then used his fluked tail to whip at the men, sending them flying against the wall.

Willa looked around. Where—

There!

The altar was on the other side of the room, a beam of light shining through the ice above them like a spotlight highlighting a humungous statue of a female looking down. Her heart pounded madly against her rib cage. Her feet moved with a mind of their own, propelling her toward the light and the Goddess.

"No!" Harken cried. "Stop her! Shoot her!"

Willa ignored the chaos around her and focused on her goal.

Goddess ... Ephyselle ... help me!

Perhaps her prayers had been answered because despite the bullets whizzing past, none of them hit her. As she neared the altar, a burst of energy hurled her forward. Holding The Wand out, she smashed it against the stone surface, breaking it into a million pieces.

A bright blast of light nearly blinded her as an invisible force propelled her backward. Warmth flooded through her, filling her up everywhere, covering her from head to toe until she was practically drowning in it. She landed on her back with a loud thud, but she felt no pain from the impact. It was hard to breathe at first, because it was like her body had suddenly grown too small to contain her.

"I ... uh ..." She gasped for breath, but managed to crawl up on her hands and knees. Slowly, when the air returned to her body, she lifted her head up.

"Willa?"

Thoralf's familiar voice made her chest burst with happiness. When her vision came back into focus and their eyes met, the strangest thing happened.

Mine, a voice in her head cried.

Thoralf staggered back, but Willa didn't miss the reply that came from deep within him.

Mine, his dragon roared back.

The warm, comforting sensation washed over Willa, but everything was happening so quickly that she didn't have time to process it.

"Willa ... you're my ..."

"Mate," she finished as she got up. "Oh, Thoralf, I—"

"You vile creatures! You will pay for this!"

They both turned to the outraged Lord Harken, whose enraged face was filled with hate.

Thoralf made a move toward him, but Willa stopped him. "No. I will take care of this evil man once and for all." She needed to do this. For her father and everyone who was lost. Closing her eyes, she called on her dragon.

It was like it had never been gone at all. She slipped into her animal's skin like she had always done—her limbs and body stretching, head elongating and growing horns. Her dragon's scales were pale blue, like ice, and resembled crystal sheets, though they were tough as armor. It let out a loud screech that reverberated through the cave.

Harken let out a scream and ran toward the passageway. The dragon of course, was much quicker and blocked his way, then opened its mouth. A gust of icy breath blew out of its maw, covering Harken. He screamed in pain as his entire body was engulfed by ice, starting with his feet and moving upward. Once his screams stopped, the temple became unnervingly silent.

"Mother Frigga!" Ranulf exclaimed.

The Ice Dragon wasn't done yet. Whipping around, it used its spiked tail to shatter the frozen statue into a million pieces. When Willa shifted back into her human form, horror struck her as the reality of what she had done sunk in.

"He deserved it," Thoralf said as he came up behind her. "Do not feel pity or regret. He hurt and killed many people—both humans and shifters. By taking his life, you have saved many."

She looked up at him, staring into those midnight blue eyes. "Just the same, I still took a life."

"You will find a way to heal from this. All of this." He took her hand. "*We* will find a way."

She believed him. In fact, she could feel him, in her heart. It was hard to describe exactly, but it was as if she knew his every emotion. His love, his faith in her, his joy—everything melding into hers. The feeling was exhilarating.

He blinked several times, then cocked his head at her.

Willa, I love you.

The sound of his voice in her head started her. *Thoralf?*

"The mating bond," he gasped aloud. "It must have formed the moment we got our dragons back."

"Formed? Doesn't that happen when mates meet?"

"Our dragons recognized each other as mates, but the bond happens later, at least from what Aleksei and the others have told me." He paused. "I think it's because we've been open and honest with each other, there was nothing blocking it."

Someone clearing their throat interrupted them. "Excuse me for intruding." It was Annika who spoke. "I wanted to let you know all is well."

"Don't apologize," Willa said. "Are you all right? And Ranulf?"

"Yes, I'm fine. Ranulf is securing Harken's goons." She nodded at the Dragon Guard who had returned to human form and was now securing them with some zip ties. "And Rorik and Niels are still unconscious but unharmed. Ranulf!" she called. "Come, let's go to that communication tower so we may inform the king of what happened."

"Thank you, Annika." She reached out and touched the female dragon's shoulder. "Thank you for everything."

"You're very welcome. And may I say, your father would have been proud of you." She covered Willa's hand and gave it a squeeze. "We will be back soon."

Once they were alone, Willa turned to Thoralf. As she gazed into his midnight eyes, warmth bloomed through her, and whether that was hers or Thoralf's emotions—or perhaps both—she couldn't tell. But it didn't matter—this was the happiest moment of her life. Not only did she have her dragon back, but now she'd found her mate too.

"Your dragon has been restored." A look of wonder passed across his face. "She's beautiful, by the way."

Her dragon preened from the compliment from its mate. Oh! How she missed that presence! "My dragon wasn't gone. Not exactly." It was hard to describe how it felt, since she had lost it long ago.

"It was just locked up inside of you." He let out a despondent huff. "I couldn't access my dragon for mere minutes ... and it was terrifying. How you managed it for years, I do not know. You are so strong, my mate."

"Mate ..." The words sounded so new to her ears, yet it felt right.

"I think I always knew," Thoralf took her hands in his. "My dragon didn't say anything because it didn't sense your dragon, but it hated being away from you."

"I—I think I knew too. From the first moment when I met you."

"I told you that I would stay—"

"As long as it takes," she finished.

A smile spread across his face. "I thought you'd forgotten."

"Never." Pulling him down, she brushed her lips over his. "I love you, Thoralf."

"And I love you."

This time he kissed her deeply, and their emotions—love, relief, joy—melded together until they were one. After all, their souls, too, were joined and would never be apart.

EPILOQUE

ONE YEAR LATER ...

"Thank you for offering to pick me up, Vera." Willa nodded at the chauffeur gratefully as he helped her into the limo, then smiled at her friend before easing into the plush leather seat.

Dark violet eyes twinkled at her. "Of course, no problem at all. Seeing as we're both going solo to this event, I thought we should go together. Besides"—she nodded at Willa's burgeoning belly—"this is more comfortable, isn't it?"

Willa laughed and then nodded at Vera's also very pregnant middle. "For you too."

"Definitely." Vera placed a hand on her stomach, then smiled wryly. "Isn't it a coincidence that today of all days, both our mates were assigned to guard King Aleksei?"

"A coincidence, I'm sure. After all, the king has much better things to do than attend the opening of the Northern Isle's first ever designer boutique."

The two women laughed.

"Stein would literally die for me, but apparently he draws the line at clothes shopping," Vera sighed.

"And Thoralf gets this look in his eyes that says he wants to go off on another three-year crusade whenever I ask him if an outfit makes my butt look fat."

"You do it on purpose."

"Of course I do."

Another peal of laughter filled the limo. In the last year, the two of them had become fast friends, mostly through their work with the Queen's Trust.

After she destroyed The Wand and bonded to Thoralf, Willa wanted to find good use for her time instead of just waiting at home all day for her mate to come home after his shift. Her Majesty suggested she look into working at the Queen's Trust, which supported many causes in the Northern Isles. So she did, volunteering with the different groups and charities under the organization's umbrella until eventually, she found her place with the Worker's Council. Thoralf had said it was the perfect place for her, having been trained to be an Alpha since birth. "Your father taught you the true meaning of being a leader—that you serve your people and put their interests first. Who better to fight for the unions and help them band together for a common cause?"

"How's the new house, by the way?" Willa asked Vera.

"Wonderful. I'm so glad they finished construction before my due date." Vera blew out a breath. "Moving while pregnant was so stressful."

Since most of the Dragon Guard were now bonded with their mates and their families were expanding, they couldn't all stay at the North Tower. So, King Aleksei found tracts of unused land in or around the Helgeskar Palace grounds where the guards who had families could build homes. Niklas and Annika didn't hesitate and were the first to start construction and eventually move out to their own estate with their large brood.

Rorik and Poppy opted to stay in the tower for now since as captain, he already had the largest apartment. Gideon and Ginny, too, preferred their flat in the tower, as they decided to wait a few more years before expanding their family, while Ranulf and Magnus, though bonded to their mates, were still technically single, so they didn't need to move out yet. Vera and Stein already had one adopted daughter, Lisbet, but as soon as Vera announced she was expecting, they made plans to build their home.

Once Willa and Thoralf found out they too were pregnant, they knew they couldn't stay in the North Tower. She initially didn't want to leave their lovely little cottage by the sea as the place had so many happy memories for her and Thoralf. They had long discussions over it, and tried to find many ways to make it work, but in the end, the choice was clear. It was a good thing too, because right before they signed off on the design, they found out even more happy news—they were expecting twins.

It was a scramble to redo the plans for two babies, and so the house wouldn't be done on time, but she knew they could manage. Still, thinking about leaving the cottage made her sad, and she just knew she would cry the day they left. But she understood that this was for the best. Besides, it wasn't like the cottage would be gone forever; King Aleksei had given it to them which meant that even if they moved, they could come back anytime.

"And how are the wedding plans going?" Vera asked, nodding at the sapphire engagement ring on Willa's left hand.

"They aren't going at all as we can't really do anything until after the children are born." Sometime after she announced her pregnancy, Thoralf had proposed. While she certainly didn't need a piece of paper to tell her he belonged to her and vice versa, she nonetheless was thrilled that he wanted to make it official. But with the house and the children, they wanted to take their time and not rush with the wedding plans.

They chatted some more as the limo made its way to the fashionable district of the city, stopping outside the about-to-be christened Maison Zaratena, the Northern Isles' first ever fashion couture house. The king's cousin, Princess Alyx, had finished her apprenticeship under a famous Parisian designer and was opening her flagship store in Odelia.

The limo door opened, and the two women alighted.

"How lovely and chic." Vera clapped her hands excitedly as she gazed at the storefront. "And I know why Alyx chose this location." Though the boutique was in the newer, trendy part of the city, the architecture stayed faithful to the old world feel of the capital. "It looks like I'm strolling into a boutique in Paris. And look at that dress." She pointed to the glass display window, which showcased a glittering gold dress on a mannequin. Behind it, the background was a sky painted with clouds.

"Beautiful," Willa gasped. "It reminds me of—"

"Queen Sybil's dragon's scales," Vera finished. "How fitting. Anyway, let's head inside. Looks like everyone's here."

Inside, the boutique was just as stylish and sophisticated as the outside—glass shelves, racks of clothing, and soft, muted lighting to showcase the beautiful dresses. However, since it was the opening, the room was packed with guests milling about, drinking champagne from crystal flutes and nibbling on canapés passed around by waitstaff in tuxes.

"Vera! Willa!"

The woman of the hour herself, Princess Alyxandria of Zaratena and the Northern Isles, and now, CEO of Maison Zaratena, came over to them. She looked fashionable as always, and today she was dressed in a short amethyst colored dress that matched her eyes and her hair and makeup perfectly done. And as always, towering right behind her was her mate and bodyguard, Ranulf. Despite his bald head covered in tattoos and beard, he looked dashingly handsome in his fitted suit.

"You're here!" she squealed, grabbing both their hands. "I'm so glad you made it."

"We wouldn't miss it for the world, Alyx." Vera hugged her and kissed her cheek. "Congratulations! The place looks fabulous."

"Thank you!" She also accepted Willa's hug. "Oh my, had I known, I would have started with a maternity line," she joked as she stared down at their bellies.

"It's not too late," Vera winked at her. "Stein is already planning the next one."

She nodded toward the buffet table. "Oh, speaking of kids, they arrived right before you."

Sure enough, all the children—Wesley, Arne, Eva, Elsie, Maya, Jakob, and Lisbet—were already feasting on the various sweets from the dessert spread, seemingly content and therefore not making any mischief.

"When Lisbet wasn't in the limo, I assumed she wasn't coming," Willa remarked.

"She wanted to ride over with her friends," Vera sighed.

"I was hoping she would at least hit her teen years before the 'mom is uncool' phase hit."

"Don't worry, she still loves you and Stein. She just wants to spend time with her friends. Come on, let's say hi."

"I should go mingle with my guests," Alyx said. "I promised Monsieur Laurent I would spend more time with his financiers."

"Go ahead," Willa urged. "And congratulations again."

They made their way to the children, who were all suspiciously whispering by the table.

"... Mama and Pappa will never find out," Maya said. "Trust me."

"They won't find out what?" Willa asked.

Eva and Elsie both let out a squeak and turned red, and the others looked around as if avoiding their gaze.

"Lady Willa!" Maya greeted as she dashed over to them, then hugged her belly. "Hello, twinsies," she said, giving her belly a kiss. "Oh, I can't wait to meet you babies." She looked up at her with those big eyes. "I'm going to be their protector."

Willa smiled down at her and winked. "I'm glad. Shifters stick together, right?"

When Willa saw the children after she had gotten her dragon back, Maya had immediately said to her, "Your dragon isn't sleeping anymore!"

Everyone had been stunned of course, because apparently the shifter children had sensed her dragon. But how could they tell that The Wand didn't destroy a shifter's animal, but simply locked it away? Annika had offered a possible explanation. "It's the innocence of children. They haven't yet been affected but the realities of the world or know what's possible or impossible. They view the world as they see it, not what others tell them."

Willa put her hands on her waist. "Have you children eaten all the desserts?"

"No," Eva said through a mouthful of eclair. "But Maya said there's always leftovers, and when the party's done, she's going to sneak—"

"Eva!" Maya hissed.

Willa laughed. "You know—"

A booming voice interrupted her. "Their Majesties, King Aleksei and Queen Sybil of the Northern Isles, Jarl and Countess of Svalterheim, Dragon Protector of the Eight Seas, The Great Firebreather ..."

Willa and Vera looked at each other as the king and queen were announced. "I thought only Queen Sybil was attending?"

"That's what I thought too," Vera said.

The king and queen entered, but that wasn't what caught the attention of the two women. It was the two men following behind them, dressed in their finest armor. Willa's dragon did a little flip inside her as did her heart as her gaze landed on Thoralf. From the look on Vera's face, she was having a similar reaction to seeing her mate.

"Come." Willa entwined her arm through Vera's. "Let's go say hi."

Thankfully the guest-list to the event was small, and mostly Alyx's family and friends, so they didn't have to wait too long to speak with the king and queen.

"Your Majesties," Vera greeted as they curtseyed. "King Aleksei, what a surprise seeing you here. I heard you had some other matters to attend to." She shot her mate a mischievous look. The stolid Stein remained stony-faced, of course, and so she continued chatting with the king and queen.

Willa, however, couldn't help but tease him through the mind link she now shared with all the Dragon Guard. *She can't wait to tell you all about Alyx's designs, and how she blended influences from current Parisian couture trends and classic Northern Isles fashion. I'm sure you're excited to hear all about it.*

Thoralf barked out a laugh, but quickly suppressed it with a cough. Stein, on the other hand, groaned through their mind link.

She turned to her mate. *Alyx has some designs she wants me to look at for my wedding dress. I'll show them to you tonight.*

This time, it was Stein who reacted—at least for him it was a reaction—as the corner of his mouth quirked up.

"... And that dress out front, have you seen it? How gorgeous." Vera placed a hand over her chest. "Did you know she was making that, Your Majesty?"

"I was as surprised as you were," Queen Sybil replied. "I was really touched by the gesture."

"Alyx said it was to commemorate the day she saved all of us," King Aleksei added. "I think it's marvelous and have asked her to preserve it so we may display it at the National Museum."

"It was a touching tribute." Vera smiled warmly. "Where are the prince and princess, by the way?"

"With their grandfather, of course," the queen said. "I swear, he spoils them too much. He dotes on Anastasia and acts like she hung the moon. And Alric!" She slapped a hand on her forehead. "Ever since Pappa started taking him flying on his dragon, it's all Alric wants to do now. I can't wait for Alric's dragon to start manifesting. At least I know he'll be able to heal from any injuries."

"Pappa would never let anything happen to Alric; you know that." The king kissed her cheek. "Besides, you might regret what you just said about his dragon manifesting."

"My father couldn't stop me from flying off every chance I got," Willa confessed.

The queen sighed. "At least you two will have a few years before you start having to tether your children to the ground."

"I wasn't *that* bad," Willa laughed. "And—" A sharp, shooting pain made her gasp. *Thoralf!*

"Willa?" He was by her side in an instant, hand clutching hers. "What's wrong? The babies?"

"I—ohh!" Something wet splashed on her shoes. "I ... I think my water just broke."

"But it's too early," he cried. "You still have at least a month to go ..."

The queen smiled gently. "Babies don't really care about calendars, I'm afraid."

"Thoralf, you must take your mate away at once," the king insisted.

I will stay and guard the king and queen. It will be fine. Stein assured him.

Vera fished her phone out of her purse. "I'll call the midwife."

"Don't make a fuss," Willa pleaded. "I don't want to ruin Alyx's big day."

"We'll make sure everything goes perfectly," Queen Sybil assured her. "Now go! We'll come by as soon as we can."

Quietly, Thoralf ushered her out of the boutique, then

Cloaked them as he shifted and lifted her to the skies. Her dragon protested, but she shushed it. *We can't fly in our condition,* she explained. *And I need you to focus and help me deliver our babies.*

Soon, they landed outside the cottage and Thoralf rushed her into the bedroom. When they were discussing birthing plans, they both agreed they wanted their children born here, in the same place Thoralf had been born in. Though birthing twins usually was higher risk, being a shifter meant she could heal from any injury, but they did consult a doctor and recruited the services of a reputable midwife.

"How are you feeling?" Thoralf asked as he helped her ease onto the bed.

"I'm fi—yeow!" she yelped as a contraction rippled up her spine.

Thoralf turned pale. "Oh gods ..."

"Thoralf, it's fine." She reached out and cupped his cheek. "This is normal, remember?"

He swallowed. "I ... yes. Sorry, I should be the one reassuring you."

Feeling his worry, anxiety, and fear through their bond, she countered it by pushing all her love and excitement back at him. "I'm ready. We both are."

"We are here."

They both turned to the door, where Annika stood. As per their plan, the moment Willa went into labor, either Annika or Niklas would fly the midwife to the cottage.

"Thank you," she said to the Air Dragon, who nodded her reply as she stepped aside to let the midwife in. She turned to Thoralf. "Let's do this."

Four hours later, Willa and Thoralf's twin son and daughter were born.

"They're beautiful!" The midwife exclaimed as she handed the children to Thoralf.

His eyes widened. "I d-don't want to drop them."

"You won't," the old woman assured him she placed them into his arms. "See? You're a natural. Now, I'll give you some privacy."

Thoralf gingerly walked back to Willa's side, kneeling down to place the pink bundle into the crook of her left arm. "Our daughter," he said reverently.

"She's gorgeous," she choked, barely keeping the tears in. "And so small." Her dragon rumbled in pride, seeing the beautiful little creature that was half hers, half her mate's.

"She'll be big and strong like her mother."

"And so will he." She nodded at the blue bundle in his arms.

He knelt down and placed their son next to their daughter. "Thank you, Willa." He leaned over to kiss her forehead.

Willa didn't need to ask him what for—she could feel his gratitude and love and joy through their bond.

"Thank you," she replied and she didn't need an explanation either. In fact, they didn't need to exchange any more words as they simply watched their newborn children, marveling in their presence. Willa couldn't help but think of the circumstances that brought her here. Yes, they were terrible and the grief would always be there, that ball hitting that button every once in a while. How she wished her father was here to meet her son and daughter, but then they wouldn't even exist if the Knights hadn't attacked and taken away her dragon. She thought of them every day, especially her father, and once in a while, her heart still felt torn that she had this wonderful new life and they were gone.

"Do not fret, my mate." Reaching over, he took her hand into his. "Enjoy this moment, it will never happen again. He would have wanted you to have this."

"I know but ..."

He kissed her palm. "We will say a prayer to the gods and the Goddess for them. For what you have lost."

"And one of thanks, for what I have now." She looked back at the children, her heart filling with so much love.

"And we must pray for Ephyselle, too." A wry smile touched his lips. "Did I ever tell you that I always suspected you were her descendant?"

"Really?"

He nodded. "It made sense to me, and I just had this feeling. That's why I wanted you to read her entire story and not skip any of the parts. Not even the sad ones."

"I'm glad I didn't." She glanced back at the twins. "What do you think they are? Ice or Water dragon?"

"I don't know, we could have one of each."

Her jaw dropped open. "Is that even possible?"

"As I learned this last year, almost anything is possible. And who knows? One day, our children could rebuild the Ice Dragon clan."

She looked into his deep midnight blue eyes, basking in the love she felt in them, even without the help of the mate bond. "True."

But for now, Willa was happy—truly happy—and content with her beautiful children and her fated mate.

Dear Reader,

Thank you so much for coming on this journey with me! It has been a pleasure to write this series, I hope you enjoyed reading it as much as I have writing it.

But this isn't the end!

But if you've read all the other books, you might be wondering ...

What's next?

Why don't you tell me?

I love hearing from readers. Email me at alicia@aliciamontgomery.com and let me know whose story you want to read next!

Maybe you want to see Matthias Thorne get his happy ending?

Or maybe a certain sexy broody Greek wolf?

I'd love to hear it.

Thanks again for reading!

Alicia

ABOUT THE AUTHOR

Alicia Montgomery has always dreamed of becoming a romance novel writer. She started writing down her stories in now long-forgotten diaries and notebooks, never thinking that her dream would come true. After taking the well-worn path to a stable career, she is now plunging into the world of self-publishing.

 facebook.com/aliciamontgomeryauthor

 twitter.com/amontromance

 bookbub.com/authors/alicia-montgomery

Printed in the USA
CPSIA information can be obtained
at www.ICGtesting.com
LVHW031146261023
762201LV00015B/2019